From The Chicken House

We all know the truth, don't we? If you go down to the woods – the animals are not going to make you tea and toast! Especially if the beasts are rather unexpected, a tiny bit dangerous, and you have to look after them/save the species/deal with horrible rogues. Veronica Cossanteli's world is outstandingly bonkers and really wild fun. (By the way, you should know she keeps pet snakes and writes with a lizard on her head. It's true!)

Barry Cunningham
Publisher

THE EXTINCTS

Veronica Cossanteli

Illustrated by Steve Wells

DEDICATION FROM VERONICA COSSANTELI:
In memory of my father,
King of the Jade Forest,
Who taught me the importance of dragons.
For my mother,
Who taught me a great many other things,
And for Xander,
Who taught me what not to write.

With thanks to all the people at Chicken House for not being too squeamish,
and especially to Rachel L, kindest and most soothing of Axe-Women,
unfailingly patient in the face of some truly terrible jokes.

Text © Veronica Cossanteli 2013
Illustrations © Steve Wells 2013
First published in Great Britain in 2013
The Chicken House
2 Palmer Street
Frome, Somerset BA11 1DS
United Kingdom
www.doublecluck.com

Cover design and illustrations by Steve Wells
Inside design and illustrations by Steve Wells
Printed and bound in Great Britain by CPI Group (UK) Ltd, Croydon,
CR0 4YY

The paper used in this Chicken House book is made from wood grown in
sustainable forests.

1 3 5 7 9 10 8 6 4 2

British Library Cataloguing in Publication data available.

ISBN 978-1-908435-45-3

Something unusual
is happening
in Wyvern
Chase Woods.
As George is soon
to find out . . .

is that
true?

Dunno
!

CHAPTER ONE

The weird stuff all began with £3.72.

I didn't know it was £3.72, of course, until I picked it up – a scattering of coins on a wet pavement – and counted it.

George Drake, it's your lucky day! Three strikes at Bumper Bowl with Josh and Matt – and now FREE MONEY! I let the coins trickle out of my hand, into my pocket, and got back on my bike.

What do you do with £3.72? Easy. If you're me, you buy sweets.

I was in the shop for about a minute. When I came out, my bike had gone. I had a paper bag full of gummy caterpillars and strawberry laces and foam bananas – but no bike. And it was raining. And it was a long walk home.

Sorry, George Drake, just kidding. Not your lucky day after all.

Great. Just great. I bit the head off a gummy caterpillar, and started walking.

By the time I got home, I was feeling a bit sick. I'm not totally sure that I like foam bananas. Mum was upside down in the garden. Other people don't do yoga in the garden in the rain, just Mum.

'Electricity bill's come,' she said, from between her knees. 'Even bigger than last time. Huge. Seriously, George – it's MONSTROUS!'

Mum only does yoga when she's worried about something. Bills. The washing machine breaking down. Parents' Evening. Dad leaving. She unfolded herself, balancing on one leg, like a flamingo – except flamingos can do it without wobbling. Then she noticed.

'Where's your bike?'

I told her, then wished that I hadn't. A good mother would have agreed that all bike thieves should be nibbled to death by flesh-eating cockroaches, or lowered head first into barrels of boiling custard, or shot into space out of giant cannons. But no – apparently, it was all *my* fault.

'You left your bike outside the shop without locking it? George, that was stupid. What were you thinking?'

Then I had to listen to a whole load of yabber-yabber-blah-blah parenty stuff about Being More Careful. It went on and on for ages, until she lost her balance and fell into a rose bush.

I pulled her out, scratched and bleeding.

'You were saying? About being *careful*?'

'Oh. Yes. Well ...' Mum sucked the blood from her fingers.

'We'll say no more about it. Stuff happens.'

Half an hour later, I was taking my mind off my lost bike with a game of *All Star Zombie Smackdown*. I was just about to poke the eyeballs out of a zombie who looked a lot like my teacher, Miss Thripps, when I heard Mum calling my name.

'George? George!'

'Just a minute. Wait—'

Too late. Miss Thripps had chewed my arm off. I called her the rudest name I could think of, and pressed Pause.

Mum was outside the back door.

'Look!' she said, proudly. 'It was right at the back of the shed. A perfectly good bike.' She brushed a cobweb off the rusting handlebars. 'Nothing wrong with it.'

Except it was pink.

Typical Mum. She's famous for forgetting things, but you'd think she'd remember ...

'Mum, I'm a *boy*.'

'Oh, that! That's all poppycock.' Mum flapped her hands. 'Real men aren't afraid of pink.'

What does Mum know about Real Men? She married Dad.

Until about a year ago, Dad lived with us. He wore a suit and tie, and went to the office every day. Now he's on a beach in Australia, wearing flowery shorts and flip-flops. He sent an email. It said the weather in Australia was lovely, and he was learning how to surf. Mum emailed him back. She said the weather in England was rubbish, and she hoped he got eaten by a shark. They're very mature for their ages, my parents. Not.

I looked at the bike. No gears. No suspension. No anything, unless you counted a rusty Princess PrettyPants bell and a little wicker basket. I tried to imagine riding that around town on a Saturday afternoon. I could picture Josh and Matt's faces ...

'No! No, Mum, I can't!'

She looked hurt, which made me feel bad. Why do grown-ups never see things? Things that are perfectly obvious? Is there a part of the brain that stops working when you get to twenty-one or something? That's a bit scary. It means I have ten years left of being normal ...

'If you want a new bike, you'll have to save up for it.' Now she was in a mood. 'I don't know how I'm going to pay that electricity bill as it is.'

Mum has a shop. It's called The Mermaid's Cave. She burns incense and plays whale music and never has any customers. I think people already have as many smelly candles and bead curtains and wind chimes as they want.

'You can earn some money,' she suggested, a bit less grumpily. 'You can wash the car. I'll give you 50p.'

'Mum, we haven't *got* a car.'

It was sold, after Dad left. We needed the money.

'I forgot.' Mum stroked the old bike's saddle. I really, really hoped she wasn't going to cry. 'Are you sure this wouldn't do? Harry and Frank both rode it.'

'Yes,' I agreed. 'But Harry and Frank are both girls.'

My sisters are older than me, but not so old that they have Grown-up Brain Rot yet. They can be really annoying, but they did see why I couldn't ride a pink Princess PrettyPants bike.

'Get a paper round,' suggested Harry. She was spraying herself silver for an Aliens and Robots party. Harry goes to college, and some very odd parties. 'I had a paper round when I was your age. I needed the cash. Mum didn't understand about my needing hair straighteners.'

Harry has loads of hair. When she isn't silver, she looks like Rapunzel, or one of those cartoon princesses. Except she has Super Mario tattooed on her bottom, and a tongue piercing, which princesses mostly don't.

'If you promise not to do anything stupid,' said Frank, 'you can work for me.'

Frank looks less like a princess. More like an owl. She's saving up to go to the Antarctic, to look after penguins, and has her own dog-walking business.

'I've got heaps of revision, and my science project to finish,' she went on. 'I could do with some help. There'll be Terms and Conditions, obviously.'

The Terms and Conditions, which Frank printed out and made me sign, meant that:

a) She kept half the money I earned.

b) I had to go to the shop for chocolate and/or cheese and onion crisps whenever she wanted.

c) I had to clean her gerbil out once a week.

The gerbil used to be called Gerald. Then we got to know him. Now he's called Dracula. He has very sharp teeth. And he doesn't like being cleaned out. But I needed the money.

The sign above the Sweet Shop door actually says 'Filling & Dentcher's Corner Emporium: Whatever You Want, We've Got It'. Because they have tall glass jars of every kind of sweet, and weigh them out for you in little paper bags, everyone just calls it the Sweet Shop. I was there on a Cheese and Onion Crisp Mission for Frank when I noticed the card in the window. Written in squiggly green writing, it was tucked in between an ad for a used toaster ('Nearly works, bargain price') and a blurry photo of a fat tabby with white paws ('Have you seen Snuffy? £100 Reward'):

HELP WANTED
INTEREST IN WILDLIFE NECESSARY
MUST BE THE RIGHT PERSON
APPLY TO MRS LIND, WORMESTALL FARM
NO SQUAMOPHOBES

I looked at it for quite a long time, until I knew the words off by heart.

I had to wait to pay for the crisps. Crazy Daisy was buying her Lottery tickets. Daisy has bright, beady eyes and hair like rice noodles under a woolly hat with ear flaps, which she wears all the time, even in summer. She lives on a bench in the park with her little dog, Doom, and shouts at people about it being the End of the World. Sometimes they throw her their spare change. She spends it all on the Lottery. I don't know why. What's the point of winning a million pounds, if the world's about to end?

Daisy was paying for three Lottery tickets and an egg sandwich, counting out pennies and 2p coins, one by one. It was going to be a long wait. I had nothing else to do, so I read the front page of the Squermington Echo.

Nothing much happens in Squermington. *Public Toilets Closed For Redecoration.* So what? *Gorgeous Gardens Competition.* Yawn. *Missing pets! Pet-nap Gang At Large? Police Warn Pet Owners To Be On Their Guard.* They were welcome to gerbil-nap Dracula, nasty, bitey little hairball: the sooner the better. *Giant Reptile Sighted! Is this the return of the Squermington Wyrm? Full story on page 3 ...*

Now that was more like it. I turned to page 3:

Miss Holly Sparrow and her friend, Miss Ruby Jenkins, claim to have seen the tail end of a very large snake-like animal as they were passing Squermington Library on their way home from the cinema on Friday night.

'We only saw the tail,' said Holly. 'But it was massive. Awesome. Ruby nearly wet herself, she was that scared. Then it sort of slithered off behind the fish and chip shop, and we ran away.'

No large animals have been reported missing from any zoos, pet shops or wildlife parks.

Could this mystery animal have anything to do with the legend of the Squermington Wyrm, the ferocious, flesh-eating monster that had local people living in terror more than a thousand years ago?

'Are you going to buy that newspaper, or what?'

Behind the counter, Mrs Filling was glaring at me. I put the paper back on the rack, and paid for Frank's crisps. Out on the pavement again, I took one last look at the Help Wanted card, and frowned. I was sure it had been written in green ink. A trick of the light, maybe. Either that or I was going mad. Because, now, that loopy, spidery handwriting was most definitely purple.

'There'll be fire and brimstone and plagues of frogs and we're all doomed,' said a hoarse voice behind me. There was a strong smell of hard-boiled egg. Daisy was feeding bits of sandwich to Doom. 'You'll see. It's The End.'

But Daisy was wrong. It was just the beginning.

'What's a squamophobe?' I asked at supper. It was Leftover Broccoli and Baked Bean Thing again. When Dad left, Mum became a herbivore. She murders helpless vegetables and makes us eat them.

Nobody knew what a squamophobe was.

'And where's Wormestall Farm?'

'In the middle of nowhere,' said Mum. 'The other side of Wyvern Chase Woods. Why?'

I explained about the card in the Sweet Shop window.

Help Wanted. Must be the Right Person.

'You're not going all that way on your own,' said Mum. 'Not through those woods. Take one of your sisters.'

'Party,' said Harry, with her mouth full. 'It's fancy dress. I'm going as a tarantula. Lots of legs to make, so I can't be disturbed.'

'I've got homework,' said Frank. 'And you're working for me this weekend, remember?' She jabbed me with her fork. 'Sir Crispin needs walking, and I have a history essay to hand in on Monday.'

'Not Sir Crispin!' I made a face. Sir Crispin is Mrs Poker-Peagrim's pug. Mrs Poker-Peagrim lives down the road from us. She has iron hair and a square face, and smells of cough sweets. Sir Crispin's so fat his fur hardly joins up around his middle, and he snores all the time, even when he's awake. His eyes bulge in a squeezed-frog sort of way. If I was going to choose a dog of my own, I wouldn't choose Sir Crispin.

I very nearly did get a dog, once. Before things got bad, and Dad went away, he said that for my eleventh birthday I could have a pet of my own. Frank had Dracula and a giant African land snail and stick insects in a jar. Harry used to have budgerigars, until she started having boyfriends instead.

'Anything you like,' said Dad. 'What do you want?'

I said I'd like a killer whale.

I'd been wanting one since the summer we went on holiday and Dad took us to Dolphin Park. Mum and the girls had gone all gooey over the dolphins. But I liked the killer whale.

You can't keep a killer whale in a semi-detached house, though. Mum and Dad argued about a lot of things, but not that.

'How about a puppy?' suggested Dad.

I said yes to the puppy – who wouldn't? – but it never happened. The arguments got louder, then Dad wasn't there any more. I got football boots for my birthday, and a new pencil case for school.

'Can't I walk Tyson instead?' I begged Frank. Tyson's a Rottweiler. That's about as close as you can get to being a killer whale and still be a dog.

'Don't be stupid,' said Frank. 'You're not big enough. And there's not much point you going to this farm place. They're hardly going to think you're the Right Person. A snotty-nosed kid?'

'My nose is not snotty. Yours is. And another thing,' I said quickly, before she could say anything back, 'what's the Squermington Wyrm?'

'What?' Mum laughed. 'That old story? Way back in the Dark Ages there was supposed to be a dragon, or some such thing, living in Wyvern Chase Woods. It ate all the cows and the sheep and the farmers' daughters, until everybody was so fed up they decided to get together one night, with their pitchforks and axes and burning torches, and hunt it down.'

'What happened? Did they kill it?'

'I've no idea. Probably some brave knight turned up on a white horse, and did it for them. That's what usually happens, isn't it? Like Saint George.'

'Yeah,' said Frank. 'I bet Saint George didn't have a snotty nose.'

'I'll tell you something,' said Mum, staring hard at my plate. 'I bet he ate his broccoli ...'

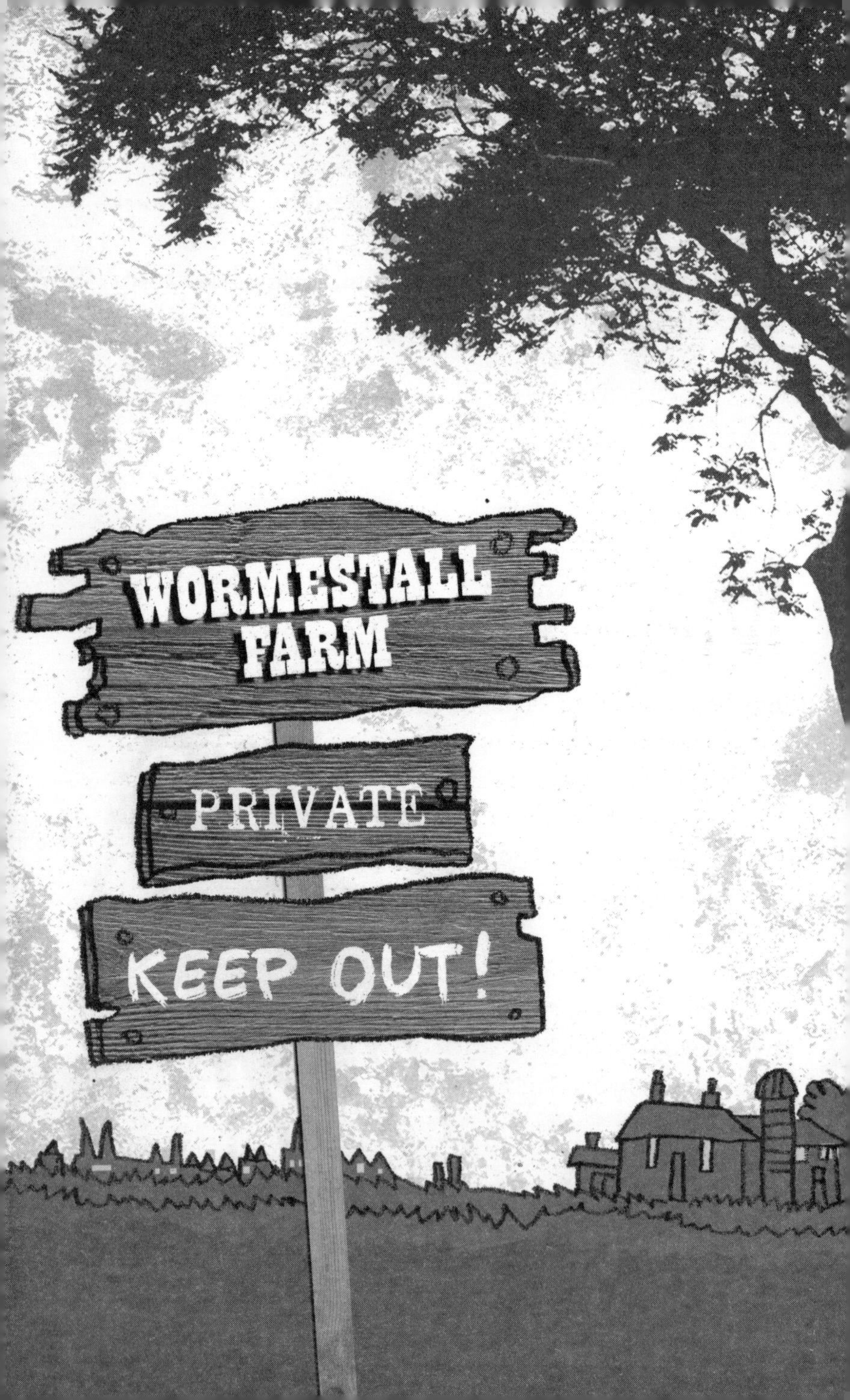
WORMESTALL
FARM
PRIVATE
KEEP OUT!

CHAPTER TWO

Mum had said not to go to Wormestall Farm by myself, so I didn't. I took Sir Crispin. Mrs Poker-Peagrim wasn't there when I went to pick him up – she was off having her hair welded or something – but Frank had told me where to find the key. Sir Crispin didn't look very pleased to see me, but I squeezed him into his little tartan coat and coaxed him out of the door. By the time we got as far as the postbox on the corner, he was ready to turn round and go home again. After that, it was more of a drag than a walk. Long before we reached Wyvern Chase Woods, I'd given up and was carrying him.

At the gate that led into the woods, I stopped. I thought about all those angry farmers. Had they marched this way with their pitchforks and their blazing torches? Had the Wyrm really had its lair here, in these woods? And what was it those two girls had actually seen, slithering around the fish and chip shop in the dark? My skin prickled, the way it does when I'm watching something scary on TV. I may have the same name as a famous dragon-slayer but, to be honest, I'm not made of hero stuff. Maybe it *is* all to do with how much broccoli you eat.

Sir Crispin whined and wriggled in my arms.

'You're right,' I told him. 'We can't stand here all day. We have to get to this Wormestall place. Before anyone else turns up and pretends to be the Right Person for the job. Because they're not. I am. Me.'

Why did I feel so sure? I don't know. I just did.

I tucked Sir Crispin under my arm, and swung open the gate.

The woods were full of stripy sunlight and squirrels and bird-twitter. Nothing scary, nothing at all.

Until something burst out of a bush right in front of me.

Sir Crispin and I both let out a yelp. It was only a bird: quite a big one, about the size of a chicken, with black and white feathers and a long neck and tail. It stared right at me for a moment, with round gold eyes and open beak, then stretched out its wings and shot off down the path. Faster and faster it tottered on bony legs, until at last it got up in the air. It didn't seem to be very good at taking off. I could hear it crashing through the branches.

When I was little, and scared of the dark, Dad used to say I had an Over-Active Imagination. Over-Active Imaginations make you see things that aren't really there; things that can't be there because they don't exist. Things like a bird with a beak full of teeth. Birds aren't supposed to have teeth ...

I walked faster after that, looking over my shoulder at every twig-snap or leaf-rustle. Which is how I stubbed my toe.

'Ow-oo-oof!'

There was a rock in the middle of the path.

'Stupid rock!'

I sat down on a tree stump, clutching my foot. Sir Crispin licked my face, all fish-breath and dribble.

'Stupid place to put a stupid rock!'

I glared at it. It stared back at me, with empty eyes. It wasn't a rock at all. It was a statue of a rabbit, carved out of stone. It was a good carving, but my toe hurt and I wasn't in the mood for Art. Who leaves a garden statue in the middle of a wood, anyway?

Standing up, I hopped about a bit until the pain wasn't so bad.

'Come on,' I said to Sir Crispin. 'You can walk the last bit. It can't be far.'

It wasn't. Soon we came out of the shadow of the trees into a narrow lane. We were away from the town, here. There were no houses or cars to be seen, just high banks full of wild flowers. A little way down the lane, a track twisted off to the right. Sir Crispin cocked his leg on a rickety wooden sign. In wobbly painted capitals, now running with yellow dog wee, it said:

WORMESTALL FARM

PRIVATE
KEEP OUT

On the other side of the track was another sign:

Beware of the

Beware of the ... what? You couldn't tell. The end had broken off.

As we turned up the track, Sir Crispin started yapping at a field full of huge, hairy cows, with dangerous-looking horns and ginger fringes. They stopped chewing and stared at us, blowing through their noses.

'I'd shut up if I were you,' I told Sir Crispin. 'I'm pretty sure that Extra-Large one in the middle is a bull.'

On our other side, a lonely horse had his nose in the hedge at the far corner of his field, twitching at flies with his tail as he munched on brambles. At the end of the track stood an old stone farmhouse. From the front, it looked blind and dead, with blank windows and little toadstools growing out of the doorstep. I knocked, but there was no answer. The door didn't look as if it had been opened for years. I was tempted to turn round and go home. But we had walked a long way, Sir Crispin and I. The card in the Sweet Shop window had told me to come here, and here I was. I wasn't giving up that easily.

I led Sir Crispin round to the back, into a cobbled stableyard. This side of the house was much more cheerful. White doves *prou-proued* in the branches of an old, gnarled tree and flowers poured from hanging baskets and window boxes. There was a jumble of boots and a row of fire extinguishers in the porch. I could hear a television on in the stable block: '... whisk the egg whites until light and fluffy ...' Somebody was watching a cookery programme.

The doorbell was an old-fashioned brass thing, with a clapper. I took a deep breath, tried hard to look like the Right Person for the job, and rang it.

The door flew open.

'Can't talk now. The De-Petrifaction Ointment's boiling,' said the old lady in the doorway, peering at me through gold-rimmed spectacles. She was wearing wellington boots and strings of beads, and an enormous hat covered in half-eaten fruit. The hallway behind her was full of pale green fog.

'Hello. I've come about the—' I coughed. The fog had reached me. My eyes began to water.

'It's a bit strong, isn't it? I'm not sure it's meant to smell like that,' said the old lady, doubtfully. 'I followed the recipe. What do you think?'

I thought it smelled like Next Door's Cat's litter tray, but I did not want to be rude, so I stuck to what I'd practised.

'I've come about the—'

'Ha! *There* you are!' said the old lady, as something greyish-brown and hairy streaked past our ankles, out of the house. 'Catch *that*,' she told me, 'and the job's yours.'

'How ...?' I began, but it was too late.

She had whisked back indoors, slamming the door shut behind her.

Sir Crispin was barking and growling.

'Shh! You're not helping!' I looped his lead around one of the fire extinguishers, to keep him out of the way. 'I'm trying to think.'

The Hairy Thing was about the same size as a guinea pig, only longer and thinner, with a pointier nose and a tail. It had squeezed itself into the gap between the house wall and a stone trough planted with flowers. I went down on my hands and knees. My hand fitted through the gap, just.

'Ow!' I whipped it out again pretty quickly. My knuckles were grazed, where they had scraped against the wall, but most of the blood – quite a lot of blood – was coming from my finger. Hairy Thing had teeth.

Sucking my finger, I decided to creep up on him from behind. I was in luck. He had wriggled so far backwards, away from my hand, that the tip of his tail was sticking out at the other end of the trough. I grabbed it, and tugged.

I tugged again.

The tail went suddenly stiff in my hands. Hairy Thing aimed his bottom at me and ... *PSSSSSSHT!*

It was the worst smell in the world – a million times worse than the old lady's green fog. Puke and dog-do and sweaty armpits and old socks and Mum's cooking, all rolled into one. And it was in my eyes, in my hair, dripping off the end of my nose ...

'Not fair,' I spluttered. 'That's cheating!'

Keeping well out of range of the Exploding Bottom, I sat

on the cobblestones and did some thinking. If I couldn't *make* the beastly, biting, stinking thing come out, I was going to have to *persuade* it out. But how?

What persuades *me* to do things I don't want to? Food, mostly.

I was wearing my favourite jeans, with the rip and the bloodstain that won't come out. I'd been wearing them for days. Which was good because when I dug about in the pockets, deep down where it's sticky, I found some escaped chocolate raisins.

I laid a trail. It wasn't a very long trail – I didn't have very many raisins. I spaced them out carefully, and waited. First, a nose came whiffling, then whiskers, liquorice eyes, twitching ears, followed by the rest of him. Hairy Thing had broken cover. Now all I had to do was catch him.

Outside the back door, there was an empty bucket. As Hairy Thing snuffled up the last chocolate raisin, I slammed it down on top of him. He was stuck.

And he wasn't happy about it. He thrashed about, sending the bucket dancing over the cobblestones. There was only one thing to do.

I sat on the bucket.

Now we were both stuck.

The sun beat down, warming the cobbles. I was hot and thirsty. To stop myself from thinking about it, I played the Million Game. It's very easy – all you have to do is count. I do it when I'm bored, or somewhere I don't want to be – like assembly or the dentist or waiting for a bus. Something un-boring always happens way before you get to a million. My record is 2,653 at Auntie Fi's wedding. I'd have got further if I hadn't lost count when the littlest bridesmaid wet her knickers. Like I said, something always happens.

I was up to 1,417 when the door opened and the old lady came out.

I pointed at the bucket underneath me. 'Got him,' I told her.

The old lady looked pleased. Several grapes and an apple core fell off her hat as she stooped to peer at something on the cobblestones. 'Blood,' she said. 'Is it yours?'

'My finger ...' I inspected Hairy Thing's teeth marks. 'It's still bleeding ...'

'Nothing wrong with bleeding,' said the old lady, cheerfully. 'It proves you're alive. It's when you *don't* bleed you should worry. But it's better not to smell of fresh blood. Not here. Come into the house. We'll find you a plaster.'

As I stood up the bucket rattled wildly. With the toe of her boot, the old lady tipped it over. Hairy Thing sat up on his haunches, chittering and furious, then shot straight up her until he reached her hat, where he settled down and started eating cherries.

'Silly Mingus,' said the old lady, fondly. 'It's not like him to run away. I think it was because of the fog in the kitchen.'

I took a quick look around. In shark-infested waters, it's a bad idea to smell of blood. I knew that. But – in a farmyard? Was there a mutant ninja sheep somewhere, sniffing the air for my blood and getting ready to attack? I jumped as something grazed my cheek. Hairy Thing was spitting cherry stones at me.

'What *is* Mingus exactly?' I asked.

'Early Mammal. Probably Triassic. He's not used to strangers,' she added as I ducked to avoid another cherry stone.

'What shall I do with Sir Crispin?' I asked. He was lying stretched out, pop-eyed and wheezy. 'I think he might need a drink of water.'

'He can come in too. All creatures are welcome at Wormestall. Except people.' The old lady gave me a sharp look over the top of her spectacles. 'Unless they come here for the Right Reasons.'

Did needing money for a new bike count as one of the Right Reasons? I hoped so.

The smell in the house was not that bad any more. The choking green fog had lifted. Sir Crispin's claws click-clacked on the flagstones as we crossed the hallway. The kitchen was like a jungle, with plants winding and trailing everywhere. There was a cat flap in the outside wall and in front of the old-fashioned cooking range was a dog bed, full of odd lumps under a rumpled tartan blanket. Sir Crispin lapped thirstily from a drinking bowl with the word DOG printed on it – except that somebody had crossed out the G and painted the letters D and O in its place.

The old lady sat me down at the big wooden table. She poured me a glass of something cold and lemony, then lifted down a box marked FIRST AID from the top of the dresser.

'We get through a lot of plasters here,' she told me. 'And bandages. And there's *that* ...' She pointed at something that looked a bit like a baseball bat, leaning against the wall. 'Emergency Wooden Leg,' she explained. 'But nobody's needed it since my Great-Aunt Hepzibah surprised a *dracunculus dentatus* in the shrubbery in 1911.'

I stared at the wooden leg, wondering what a *dracunculus dentatus* looked like. I didn't want to ask, in case she thought I was stupid. Frank always tells me I'm stupid when I don't know things.

'So, you're looking for a job,' said the old lady, mopping my finger with something that stung. The Early Mammal had gone to sleep, curled around her hat, with its paws over its nose. 'What brought you to Wormestall, I wonder?'

'The advertisement. In the Sweet Shop window.'

'Ah, so you saw it.' She screwed the top back on the stinging stuff and reached for a plaster. 'What colour was it written in?'

'Green. No – not green.' I frowned. 'Purple. I'm not sure ...'

'But you could read it, could you? Quite easily?'

I didn't know what she was getting at. Was she worried about my eyesight, or was she making sure I knew how to read?

'I can remember what it said,' I told her. 'Help wanted. Interest in wildlife necessary. Must be the Right Person. Apply to Mrs Lind, Wormestall Farm. No squa ... squam ...

squamophobes. Are you Mrs Lind?'

'I am. And do you know what a squamophobe is?'

'No,' I admitted.

'A person with a fear of scales. You don't have a problem with scales, do you?'

Fish scales? Piano scales? Weighing scales? I tried to look as if I knew what she was talking about.

'Scales are all right,' I said, carefully. 'And I'm quite interested in wildlife.'

'What sort of wildlife?' Mrs Lind wrapped the plaster around my finger. 'The cuddly, fluffy kind? Or the other sort?'

I thought of the killer whale at Dolphin Park, and Tyson the Rottweiler.

'The other sort,' I said, definitely.

Mrs Lind closed the first aid box and sat back, fingering her beads. 'I suppose you have a name?'

I nodded. 'George.'

Her brows snapped together. 'Not after that tiresome saint, I hope?'

'Saint George was OK.' I felt I had to stick up for him. 'He must have been. He killed the dragon, didn't he?'

Saint George was the Good Guy. The dragon was bad. Everyone knows that.

Mrs Lind gave a snort. 'I've never seen anything very saintly about riding around the country killing off rare animals.'

'But dragons ate people. Somebody had to kill them!'

'You think so?' Mrs Lind gave me another of those sharp looks. 'What did you have for lunch yesterday, George?'

'Er – shepherd's pie.' After Mum's vegetable experiments, even school dinners came as a relief.

'Shepherd's pie is made of sheep. So you ate a sheep, George. I expect you were hungry, were you?'

'Yes,' I said, uneasily. 'It wasn't a whole sheep—'

'I expect Saint George's dragon was hungry,' Mrs Lind interrupted me. 'For all you know, she had hatchlings – hungry hatchlings – waiting to be fed.'

I opened my mouth, then shut it again. I was getting confused. Dragons weren't real. All that stuff about St George was only a story – right?

'Actually,' I said, 'I think I was named after my grandfather.'

The fierce look died out of her eyes. 'Well, there's nothing wrong with that!' Fishing around on the brim of her hat, in between a nibbled plum and a banana skin, she found a packet of peppermints and offered me one. 'Not everybody would have been able to read that advertisement, you know. The ink it was written in was … unusual. You must be the person I was looking for.' She smiled at me. 'The Right Person.'

Yes! I couldn't wait to see Frank's face when I told her.

'I'll work hard,' I promised. 'When do I start?'

'At the Right Time,' replied Mrs Lind. 'You'll know when that is.'

CHAPTER THREE

It doesn't happen in films or books, but it happens in real life: at exactly the Wrong Time, you need to go to the toilet. Especially if you've been eating Leftover Broccoli and Baked Bean Thing.

'Up the stairs. Turn right. Down the corridor,' said Mrs Lind, when I asked. 'Second on the left. I have to go and feed the ducks. They don't like being kept waiting.' Popping a peppermint in her mouth, she adjusted her hat, and picked up a bucket. 'Let yourself out.'

Leaving Sir Crispin tied to the banister, I climbed the bare wooden staircase.

Upstairs, there wasn't much to see – the doors leading off the corridor were all closed. I found the bathroom, and locked myself in with the heavy iron key. On the wall hung a picture of an old lady in a black dress and a bad temper. I recognized her from History. Queen Victoria. She's been dead for ages: more than a hundred years. Nothing in the bathroom, by the look of it, had changed much since her day. The bath stood on legs with clawed feet, and was full of murky green water. The toilet looked as if it belonged in a museum – you had to reach up and pull a chain when you flushed. Next to it, on a low table, was a glass tank with little fish darting in and out of what looked like a real human skull.

I sat down, with my jeans around my ankles. Queen Victoria was staring at me, which put me off a bit. I twisted round to look at the little fish, black and silver and gold, whisking in and out of the skull's eye sockets. I was just trying to imagine what it would be like to have fish flicking their tails where your eyeballs should be when I felt ... what? Something cold and wet, crawling across my bare skin ... Something underneath me ... I froze, heart thudding. What What **WHAT** was I sitting on?

Slippery and damp, first one, then another long grey tentacle came snaking over the top of my leg, across my lap. They were heading for my ...

I came off that toilet like a cork out of fizzy wine. There's not much point yelling for help in a locked room when you're the one with the key. Yanking my jeans up with one hand, I was fumbling at the lock with the other when there was a sudden loud thud, right above my head. Something had crash-landed on the roof.

I thought of all the things it could be. A meteorite from outer space? An alien spaceship? Or a pigeon. Dad always used to tell this story about how he was at a party when a dead pigeon fell out of the sky and landed slap-bang in the middle of the barbecue.

Then somebody swore, loudly and rudely, the way dead pigeons definitely don't. There was a rustling of branches outside the open window. Then there was a boy.

He sat astride the window sill. About Frank's age, maybe – blue eyes, a thin, moody face, twigs in his spiky black hair, and a winged skull on his T-shirt. The day was warm, but he was wearing a heavy, hooded jacket, several sizes too big. Under his arm he held a life-sized statue of a cat, with a label around its neck.

He did not look particularly surprised to see me, hanging onto the door handle and trying to zip up my flies at the same time. 'Have you got a pen?' was all he said.

Wordless, I shook my head. The boy frowned. Digging about in his pockets, he brought out a chewed stub of pencil and scribbled something on the label.

'32 Rhododendron Road. At least, that's where I found it. Who knows where it came from? Can't tell with cats.'

Swinging his legs over the sill, he put down the cat and looked at me. His blue eyes were strangely bright, and he didn't seem to need to blink.

'What's up with you?' he asked.

I'd managed to do up my jeans at last, but my hands were still shaking.

'In there!' I pointed at the toilet. 'There's a *Thing*! It's got—' I stretched out my arms, waggling them up and down. As octopus impressions go it wasn't great, but he got it.

'Oh, that,' he said. '*That's* supposed to live in the bath. It keeps getting out. You have to be firm with it.' He grabbed the toilet brush. 'Stop messing about,' he ordered. 'You've had your fun. Now get back where you belong.'

Plunging the brush into the toilet bowl, he twisted and twirled it, winding tentacles around it like a forkful of spaghetti. He raised the brush, but the Thing refused to come. Suckering its free tentacles against the sides of the toilet bowl, it held on grimly, its eyes tight shut.

'Stupid cephalopod!' muttered the boy.

Toilet brush in one hand, he reached out the other hand towards the fish tank. Before I had time to blink, he had plucked out a fish and was dangling it, by its tail, above the toilet.

He whistled, short and sharp. The Thing opened pale, hooded eyes and fixed them on the fish.

'Come on, then.' The boy lifted the fish higher. 'What are you waiting for?'

The Thing gave in. Letting go of the toilet, it wrapped itself around the brush. The boy swung it from toilet to bath, where it plopped, like a blob of grey jelly, into the water. He threw it the fish, which it caught with one tentacle and posted into its beak of a mouth, before shuffling off to sulk under the taps.

'What *is* it?' I asked. Its body was the size and shape of a large mango. I counted the tentacles. Eight. I shuddered, remembering what they had felt like on my bare skin. 'Is it an octopus?'

'Kraken. Only a baby, but it's getting too big for the bath. This time next year it'll be the size of a garden shed. Not full-grown, of course. Not for another century.'

'A hundred years?' I stared at the kraken. It stared back at me. 'How big will it be then?'

'Have you ever been to the Isle of Wight?'

'Once.' I nodded. 'On holiday.'

'Well, about that big.' Leaning against the washbasin, with his hands in his pockets, the boy inspected me. 'What are you, anyway?'

'Me? I'm ... er ... I came about the job.'

'Numpty Numbskull's job?' The boy raised an eyebrow. 'Reckon you're up to it, do you?'

'Yes,' I said, firmly. If somebody called Numpty Numbskull was up to it, so was I. Whatever IT was. 'Mrs Lind said I was the Right Person.'

The boy shrugged. 'In that case ... She's as daft as a wet parrot sometimes, but she makes up her own mind, and it's never any use arguing. You can't be any worse than Numpty. I've known beetles with more brain than him. Didn't know the difference between February and Friday, and couldn't count past nineteen. And *that* was using all his fingers and toes.'

'Wouldn't that make twenty?'

'Not in Numpty's case,' said the boy. 'Don't make assumptions. But he was quite good at acting out Viking poetry on the kitchen table in his pyjamas. Can you do that?'

'Um, not really.'

'Oh well.' The boy hunched his shoulders. 'It used to pass the time, on a winter's evening. Can you make pine needle porridge?'

'Pine needle ...? No.'

'Pine needle soup?'

I shook my head. Perhaps I wasn't the Right Person after all.

'Pine needle fritters?'

'I could learn ...'

'Don't!' said the boy. 'They're disgusting. The whole house used to smell of burnt Christmas tree. Mrs L pretended to like them. She didn't want to hurt his feelings, but if you ask me—'

He stopped. A furious squawking was coming from downstairs.

'Dumb-cluck bird's stuck in the cat flap again. All feathers and no brain.' As he spoke, the boy tweaked another fish from the tank and tossed it into the bath.

'The poor fish!' I said, watching its tail thrash as the kraken caught it.

The boy spun round to face me, his eyes glittering and fierce.

'Listen,' he hissed. 'We have a lot of mouths to feed here. All of them like their food fresh. If you're going to get all squealy and squeamish every time somebody gets eaten, then you're really, really not the Right Person for the job—'

'I won't,' I said, quickly. 'I won't squeal, or ... or have squeams. I *am* the Right Person, I promise you. I want the job – I really do!'

'What on earth's that?' asked the boy, when he set eyes on Sir Crispin at the bottom of the stairs. 'Is it meant to look like that?'

'It's Mrs Poker-Peagrim's pug.' I untied the lead from the banister. Sir Crispin was yapping at something. A lonely feather, shiny blue-black like a magpie's wing, lay on the hall flagstones, rocking in a puff of air.

'Dumb dog!' I tugged at the lead.

The boy picked up the feather. With an odd little twitch of his shoulders, he put it in his pocket.

'He's not as dumb as you think, Mrs Poker-Peagrim's pig.'

'Not pig, *pug*.'

The boy shrugged. 'Whatever.'

At the sound of his voice, another burst of angry squawking broke out from behind a closed door. I wanted to see what sort of bird gets stuck in a cat flap, but the boy just gave the door a kick.

'Shut your beak, feather-brain!' he ordered. 'Or I'll come round behind you and poke you through that cat flap with the carving fork. I mean it – I'm hungry.'

There was silence, then a bit of bad-tempered *proop-prooping* but it wasn't very loud.

'She reckons she's safe because she's too fat to fit in the oven,' said the boy, darkly. 'But we have sharp knives and a very large saucepan. There's more than one way of cooking a bird, you know.'

Out in the stable yard, Sir Crispin hid behind my legs, whining unhappily.

'He can smell it,' said the boy.

'Smell what?' I sniffed the air.

Smoke.

Little frilly wisps of smoke were squeezing through the cracks in one of the stable doors. As I watched, the wisps darkened and thickened. I could hear crackling ... Fire.

'There's somebody in there!' I said, urgently. 'The TV was on – I heard it.'

'Only Grissel.' The boy didn't sound at all worried. 'She does it for attention. And when she wants the channel changed.'

'Who's Grissel?' I asked.

'Grissel's ... just Grissel.' He was looking up at the sky.

'But – shouldn't we do something? Ring 999?'

'What for? Anyway, no phone.'

'No *phone*?' What sort of house had no phone? 'I could go for help. I'm a fast runner. Where's the nearest house? They'll have a phone and—'

'I said no phone.' His eyes were still on the sky. 'And no people. I'll deal with it. It's better if you go.'

I looked at the fire extinguishers in the porch.

'I can help ...'

'No, you can't. You'll just get in the way. Go.'

He didn't say goodbye. He didn't even look at me. Staring upwards, he seemed to be concentrating on something I couldn't see, like someone doing a really difficult sum in their head.

As I rounded the corner of the house, I stopped and looked back. The boy still had his face turned up to the sky, his eyes fixed on the clouds. He drew his jacket around him as the first raindrops began to fall.

Clouds? Rain?

Five minutes ago, there had been nothing up there but clear blue sky. Now it was growing dark as clouds rolled in out of nowhere, blotting out the sun. The boy didn't move. Nor did I. I hardly noticed my sodden T-shirt and dripping hair as the rain came tipping down on the burning stable and the spiral of smoke grew thinner and fainter, and finally died out altogether.

It was all over, as suddenly as it had started. The boy shook himself, like a wet dog, and turned to go back into the house. By the time he closed the door behind him, the sun was shining again.

If the Squermington Wyrm had been in the woods as I walked home, I'd probably have tripped over it without even noticing. My head was full of Wormestall. I was in a hurry to get home, and check out a few things on the Internet. Things like krakens and Early Mammals, and whether anyone had ever been able to control the weather ... I wouldn't say anything to Mum or the girls. They would only laugh at me and make annoying jokes about Over-Active Imaginations. Let them go on thinking Wormestall was an ordinary farm.

It would be my secret.

CHAPTER FOUR

The week started badly. Miss Thripps was having one of her Moody Mondays. We hadn't even got through registration, and she was already moaning. 'I'm sick and tired of you boys at the back talking all the time,' she told us. 'I'm splitting you up. Joshua, go and sit next to Yasmin. Prudence – you can sit next to George.'

Prudence was new. All I knew about her was that she had red hair. I'd only noticed because Nathan had been teasing her about it, out in the playground. Not ginger. Red, like blood, with fierce, dark eyebrows that frowned a lot. The frowning may have been because of Nathan. Nathan has about three and a half brain cells. His favourite thing is making people cry: new kids, little kids, weird kids, supply teachers – anyone. He's good at it. But it hadn't worked with Prudence. Yet.

Prudence sat down beside me. I didn't look at her. She didn't look at me.

Miss Thripps shut the register with a snap.

'As this is Prudence's first day,' she said, 'I think it would be nice if she introduced herself to the class. We can practise our listening – *nicely*, Nathan – while she tells us all about herself.'

Sideways, I glanced at Prudence. She looked as if she wished she was somewhere else.

'Stand up, Prudence,' said Miss Thripps. 'So we can all see you.'

Slowly – very slowly – Prudence scraped back her chair and got to her feet.

We all looked at her, waiting.

Nothing.

'Well?' said Miss Thripps.

Prudence shrugged.

Miss Thripps's smile was dying. 'Why don't you start with your family, dear? Don't you have any brothers and sisters? What about your parents?'

'I have my mother's hair,' began Prudence, at last. 'And her eyes. That's what everybody says. I don't have any of the rest of her. She's dead. So's my dad. He was killed. By a hippopotamus.'

A ripple of interest washed through the class. You could see Miss Thripps wondering if she had made a mistake.

'Hippos are very dangerous beasts,' she said. 'Did it happen in Africa, dear?'

Prudence shook her head.

'Cromwell Road, South Kensington, London.'

Miss Thripps looked a bit surprised. Before she could say anything, Lakshmi's hand shot up in the air.

'If you haven't got a mum and you haven't got a dad, who do you live with?'

'My stepmother.' Prudence said the word 'stepmother' the same way I might say 'Brussels sprouts'. Her nose wrinkled, as if something didn't smell good. 'Diamond Pye. She's a taxidermist.'

'A taxi driver?' said Miss Thripps. 'That's a very useful thing to be. I had to take a taxi myself, just the other day, and—'

'Not a taxi driver.' Prudence interrupted her. 'A taxidermist. She stuffs things. Birds. Animals. And ... things.'

'*Eeeeww*!' said several of the girls, making faces.

'Is it dead?' asked Dean. 'The stuff she stuffs?'

Prudence nodded.

No one but me heard her add, 'By the time she's finished, it is.'

In the playground, at break, Nathan had another go at making Prudence cry.

She was leaning against the climbing frame when he barged into her, making her drop the book she was reading.

'*BLAAARGH*!' he roared, opening his mouth very wide. 'I'm going to eat you! And your dad. I'm a hippopotamus!'

Actually, he did look quite like one.

Prudence picked up her book. 'Hippopotamuses are

herbivores,' she said. 'They don't eat meat. Everybody knows that, And another thing,' she added. 'There's never been a hippopotamus nearly as ugly as you.'

'Prudence Pye! That is a very unkind thing to say!' Miss Thripps was on playground duty, stalking about, sticking her nose into other people's business and getting it all wrong, as usual. 'You've hurt poor Nathan's feelings. I think you should apologize, right now!'

Prudence shrugged. 'Sorry.' Her nose was already back in her book.

She looked as if she didn't care. She looked as if she was reading – but she can't have been because her book was upside down.

Nathan wasn't in the playground doing hippopotamus impressions at lunchtime because he was in the Head Teacher's Office, being told off. He'd been in trouble twice. The first time was for laughing at Jamie May, who was crying because his dog, Peanut, had run away and not come home. The second time was for telling Aisha and Katie that the Squermington Wyrm was hiding in the Girls' Toilets. None of the girls would go in there after that. They just huddled outside, screaming, with their legs crossed.

When the bell rang for home time, Miss Thripps kept Josh back for one of her Little Talks. He had been drawing spaceships in his Literacy book again. I was hanging around outside the school gates, waiting for him, when a car screeched to a halt beside me. Roof down, music thumping, it parked with its near wheels up on the pavement, practically running me over. I leapt backwards, squeezed up against the school railings, and stared.

The car looked fast, expensive and mean. And pink. Bright, shiny pink. You couldn't really see what the driver looked like because most of her face was hidden by her sunglasses. Her hair was long and loose and slippery – and the same colour as the car. Bright, shiny pink. She was sucking a lollipop.

The horn blared, sharply, making me jump. Then I saw Prudence. She came out of the gates, head bent, rummaging for something in her schoolbag. At the sound of the horn, she looked up and saw the car. Schoolbag hanging from her hand, she just stood there.

The woman took the lollipop out of her mouth. It was pink.

'It's like waiting for a snail,' she complained. 'Get a move on, can't you?'

'I said I'd walk.' Prudence's face was blank, like a piece of paper with nothing on it.

Pink fingernails tip-tapped on the steering wheel. 'Well, I'm here now.'

'I want to walk,' said Prudence.

'Other children – *nicer* children – would say thank you. You – that boy there!' The woman jabbed her lollipop at me. 'You'd like a ride in this car, wouldn't you?'

'Mmm,' I said. I don't really like being told what I'd like.

'Actually ... well, it's a bit *pink*.'

The woman laughed – a clinky, tinkly laugh, like the wind chimes Mum has in her shop. Wind chimes can be really annoying. 'You men,' she said. 'You're such scaredy-cats – afraid of a colour! Prudence, get in the car.' The wind chimes had stopped tinkling. 'Get in *now* – or you'll be spending the night you-know-where.'

Prudence flinched, as if someone had hit her. She got into the car. As it disappeared around the corner I noticed the number plate: STUPP U.

I wondered, just for a moment, what it was like when you didn't have a mum and your dad had been killed by a hippopotamus. Then Josh appeared, kicking his water bottle across the playground, and Prudence went out of my head.

Usually, Josh and I hang out together after school on a Monday. Today it was different: he was going to Matt's house. They were going to mess around on their bikes. Matt had a new bike – gleaming black and silver, with about a million gears. He could ride it with no hands and you could see him thinking he was the coolest thing on the planet. They were going to look for lost pets. Half the pets in Squermington seemed to be missing. There were posters up everywhere, offering rewards. Jamie's dad was offering £100 for Peanut.

'We're starting a Lost Pet Detective Agency,' said Josh.

'And you're not in it,' added Matt, 'because you haven't got a bike.'

Mum was in the kitchen when I got home. The Mermaid's Cave doesn't open on Mondays. Never any customers on a Monday, says Mum. Never any customers on a Tuesday, Wednesday, Thursday, Friday or Saturday either. But nobody says that out loud.

The washing machine had broken down. Again. There was a flood in the kitchen, with Mum standing on one leg in the middle of it, doing her flamingo thing. Her eyes were closed and the palms of her hands were pressed together above her head.

Yoga's OK, I suppose, but sometimes what you really need is the Washing Machine Fix-it Man.

'Mum?' I stayed in the doorway, on dry land. 'Have you called the Fix-it Man?'

She opened one eye, then shut it again. 'The Fix-it Man costs money. We can't afford him. Not again.'

'Oh.' I looked at the dirty grey suds swirling around the floor. Next Door's Cat was marooned on the ironing board. 'Where's all the water going to go?'

'Shh,' said Mum. 'I'm breathing.'

I had nothing to do. I didn't even have Sir Crispin to walk any more.

'Due to your irresponsible behaviour,' Frank had told me, 'I have no option but to terminate your employment.'

'What?'

'You're sacked, stupid.'

Mrs Poker-Peagrim had complained. She said I couldn't be trusted with the care of a sensitive, highly bred animal. I had kept Sir Crispin out too long, and made him walk too far. He might have had a heart attack. I pointed out that as I'd carried the fat fur-bag most of the way, if anyone had a heart attack it was more likely to be me.

'Doesn't matter,' said Frank. 'I've finished my essay. And my science. I don't need you any more. You're redundant.'

She gave me 83p redundancy money, which (she said) was kind of her. I put it in the shoebox under my bed marked 'EMERGENCY BIKE FUND – EXTREMELY URGENT!!!' But it wasn't going to get me very far.

It was the Right Time to go back to Wormestall Farm.

'Mum? I'm going out.'

'You've only just got in! Have you done all your homework?'

'Mmm.' Sort of true. RE doesn't count.

'All right, then. Don't be late back.'

I did feel a tiny bit guilty, leaving her alone in her puddle. Honestly, if Dad had to take tests in being a dad and a husband, he'd hardly get any marks at all. I'd just about forgiven him for not letting me have a killer whale, but he could have bought Mum a new washing machine before he left.

CHAPTER FIVE

As I turned up the track towards Wormestall Farm, the horned cows were chewing peacefully. The bull lifted his heavy head to watch me, licking his nose with a meaty pink tongue. He must have decided that I wasn't worth bothering about because he went back to eating grass. The horse had his back to me, with his nose in the hedge again.

I was about to clang the bell when I saw the scrap of paper pinned to the door:

Back soon. Biscuits in kitchen. Mind the eggs.

I wasn't sure what to do. Was the note meant for me? They didn't know I was coming. On the other hand, who else were they expecting? People were not welcome at Wormestall – Mrs Lind had said so.

The bit about biscuits reminded me that I was hungry. Whoever that note was really for, surely they wouldn't care if I ate just one biscuit?

The door swung open easily. As I crossed the hall, I glanced up the stairs, remembering my trip to the bathroom. According to the Internet, the kraken is a legendary sea monster which doesn't really exist. Clearly, the Internet was wrong. Admittedly, the Wormestall kraken was more of a legendary toilet monster.

'Ouch!' Not looking where I was going, I had stubbed my toe.

'Not *you* again!' I said. It was the stone rabbit. I was positive it was the same one. 'What are you doing here?'

Limping into the kitchen, I found a jug of lemonade, chinking with ice, on the table. Stuck to the biscuit tin was another note: Help Yourself. So I did.

With a glass in one hand and a biscuit in the other, I wandered around the kitchen, being nosy. There was a very large saucepan on the hob. I peeped inside.

'Yuck!' I slammed the lid back on quickly. The pan was full of stinking green slime.

The Emergency Wooden Leg was in its corner by the door, and a note stuck to the fridge said Lo, don't forget to squeeze the weasel. Apart from that, everything seemed normal enough. There were jam jars full of flowers, and a rocking chair, and cheerful yellow-checked curtains blowing in the breeze through the open window. And that dog bed. Who slept in it? And why was it so lumpy?

I was just prodding one of the lumps with the toe of my trainer when something hurtled through the cat flap like a feathered cannonball, hitting the back of my knees and knocking my feet out from under me. Half a glass of lemonade and the remains of a chocolate chip cookie flew through the air as I went over backwards.

Various bits of me hurt, quite a lot. I shut my eyes. Then I found I couldn't breathe, so I opened them again.

An angry bird with a fat body, stubby little wings, tufts of grey feathers and a big, curved beak was standing on my stomach, pecking at my nose and glaring at me with mad orange eyes.

'Ow!' I said, faintly, putting up my hands to protect my nose.

'Dido, you bad bird!' Mrs Lind was standing in the doorway with an odd-shaped bundle in her hands. She was still wearing her wellies and her beads, and the Early Mammal was perched on her hat, cleaning bits of banana off his whiskers. 'Get off!'

'I told you!' The boy had appeared at Mrs Lind's shoulder. 'She'd be a lot less annoying if we cooked her.'

Dido hopped off my stomach. Letting go of my nose, I propped myself up on my elbows, but the relief didn't last. Now she was attacking my ankles. I kicked out at her, but it wasn't any use. This bird had problems with Anger Management.

'What we need,' said the boy, pensively, 'is a good recipe for Bird Vindaloo.'

Mrs Lind clicked her tongue. 'Hold that,' she told me, handing me her parcel, then she flung herself, in a sort of rugby tackle, on top of the bird. 'There now.' Panting slightly, she tucked it, squawking, under her arm. 'She doesn't really mean any harm.' She looked at my bruised nose and bleeding ankles. 'Did you touch her eggs?'

'Eggs?' I looked at the dog bed. Beneath the edge of the blanket, I could make out something pale. 'Oh. *That's* what the lumps are.'

'She takes her Egg-Sitting very seriously,' explained Mrs Lind. 'I'm sorry we weren't here when you arrived. We were up in the barn. Crackling Rose had her piglets today. Twelve of them. That one's the runt.'

I looked down at the parcel in my lap. A pig. A tiny black piglet, wrapped up in a towel.

'Pigs-in-blankets,' said the boy, hungrily. 'Sausage roll. Toad-in-the-hole. Suckling pig, with—'

'This is Lo,' Mrs Lind told me, interrupting him. 'Short for Lobelius. It's not his real name, but I have to call him something and that's what I was doing when he came out of nowhere – planting lobelia. Blue, like his eyes. He likes you to think he doesn't care about anything, but it isn't true. He's a great help to me, although it makes him very cross when I say so. And he *hates* it if you use the A-word.'

'What's the A-word?' I asked.

'Absolutely-none-of-your-business, that's what.' Lo yawned, showing very white teeth. He might be named after a flower, but nobody in their right mind was going to give this boy a hard time about it. 'We've already met,' he informed Mrs Lind. 'In the bathroom. The kraken was trying to give him a cuddle.'

'Oh dear,' said Mrs Lind, guiltily. 'Sorry, George. I should have warned you. I'm afraid the poor thing gets bored, all by itself in that bath. Would you like to give the pig its bottle? I'll warm up some milk.'

As she set Dido down on the floor, I scrambled to my feet. Clutching the piglet, I edged around the table, away from that wicked beak.

I'm not great on birds: I can tell an owl from an ostrich and a parrot from a penguin, and that's about it. But now I looked at this bird properly, I knew I'd seen it before – in a glass case, in the Natural History Museum. You couldn't mistake it: it looked like a turkey crossed with a feather duster.

I stared. 'Isn't that …? That's a dodo! Shouldn't she be … extinct?'

The boy laughed. Mrs Lind put her finger to her lips. 'We don't use that word here, George. The E-word.'

'*You* don't. I do.' Lo helped himself to a cherry off Mrs Lind's hat, flicking the stone at Dido. 'Extinct. Extinct. You stink. You'd smell better in a curry.'

The bird glared at him, snapping her beak.

'Dido is the only dodo left that we know of,' said Mrs Lind, sadly. 'There were never very many to start with, and they were all on one island. I'm afraid they were too trusting, and too easy to catch.'

'Proof,' said the boy, 'that it doesn't pay to be nice. While the other dodos were clucking about in the open, being stupidly friendly and getting eaten, Dido's lot hid behind a bush and sulked. Saved by their own bad temper.'

With an evil look at Lo, the bird waddled over to her dog bed. Twitching back the tartan blanket with her beak, she inspected the clutch of eggs nestling underneath it: creamy white, buttery yellow, freckled green, all different shapes and sizes. The biggest was enormous, the size of a watermelon.

'She never laid that!' I'm no eggs-pert (ha ha!) but even I could see that it was several sizes too large.

'She didn't lay any of them,' said Mrs Lind. 'That one came in the post. The parcel was marked "Fertile". The Post Office read it as "Fragile" and managed not to break it, which was lucky. We have no idea what's inside. We don't know what any of them are, until they hatch.'

'*If* they hatch,' the boy corrected her. 'She's been sitting on some of those for years. They're probably rotten by now. One of these days they'll break, and the stink is going to make your eyes water.'

Mrs Lind was pouring milk into a baby's bottle. She tested the temperature, then handed it to me. 'You had better sit down – no, not *there*!'

She spoke too late. I was lowering myself into the rocking chair, and my bottom had already made contact with the top cushion. At least, I thought it was a cushion – covered in blue and yellow stripes – until it let out a muffled squelch, like a punctured water balloon, and slithered out from under me. Holding the end of its tail in its mouth, it dragged itself sideways under the table, where it lost its stripes and turned the same colour as the flagstones.

'Show some respect,' said Lo. 'You nearly sat on Tail-biter.'

'Sorry,' I said. 'I didn't know it was there. Er – what is it? And what's it doing?' Curled in a circle – half-reptile, half-doughnut – it still hadn't let go of its tail.

'It's representing eternity,' said Mrs Lind, with a sigh. 'Not really very sensible, but it's an ouroboros and that's what they do. It makes it very difficult to feed, and it gives itself terrible sores, sucking its tail like that, but it's afflicted by a sense of duty. It believes that if it ever lets go and breaks the circle, Time will stop.'

'Would it?' I asked. 'Would Time stop?'

'We don't know,' said Mrs Lind. 'It's never happened.' She gave the rocking chair a brush with her hand. 'Look at that,' she complained. 'Scales all over the furniture. You're not allergic, are you, George? It used to make poor Numpty sneeze so.'

Numpty Numbskull, who didn't work there any more.

'Was that why he left?'

'Who said anything about him leaving?' Lo pulled a custard cream apart, throwing Dido the half with no cream. She caught it in her beak with a snap. 'He's upstairs, in the cupboard.'

'For safe keeping,' explained Mrs Lind. 'But you'll do very well in his place,

George. You have a way with animals.'

'Do I?' I rubbed my sore nose.

'You caught Mingus, didn't you? And Dido could easily have pecked your eyes out, if she didn't like you. She bit off one of Numpty's toes. I did warn him about walking around barefoot.'

'It's still in the fridge,' said Lo. 'The toe.'

'You shouldn't throw away people's toes,' said Mrs Lind. 'Not without asking.'

The hungry piglet quickly got the hang of the bottle, and was soon slurping noisily on my lap. Dido perched on top of her egg collection, with her feathers fluffed out and her eyes half-closed. Mingus was snoring on Mrs Lind's hat. Tail-biter stayed under the table, watching me with emerald-eyed suspicion.

'Where do they all come from?' I asked. 'How do they get here?'

'The world is running out of hiding places for anything that doesn't want to be found,' said Mrs Lind, sadly. 'Humans are taking up too much space, cutting down the forests, blasting through the mountains, poisoning the water. Creatures lose their homes; they have nowhere else to go. Sometimes they're Lingerlings, like Mingus and Dido, left behind when the rest of their species dies out. Others are Cryptids, like Tail-biter and the kraken. People say these animals don't exist ... They keep out of sight, away from human eyes. One way or another, many of them make their way here. We never know when they'll arrive – or how. Sometimes they're born here. Like that piglet. You had better turn it round now, George, while there's still some milk left. The other end will want a turn.'

I stared at her, then down at the pig. The other end? Cautiously, I unwrapped the towel. I was getting used to Wormestall. It wasn't that much of a surprise. The piglet had a head at both ends.

'Ping Feng,' said Mrs Lind. 'They're Chinese.'

'Sweet and sour pork,' said Lo, licking his lips. 'The question is, which end is which?'

'Don't listen to Lo,' Mrs Lind told me. 'He doesn't mean it. George – I have to ask you not to talk about what you have seen here. If people ever found out – well, there would be a fuss. They would want to take the animals away, and put them in zoos or laboratories or ... or something even worse. We've already lost one. We have to keep the others safe. Do you understand?'

I nodded. 'I won't say anything. You can trust me.' I meant it. I would not betray the animals of Wormestall Farm. Not ever. I remembered the headlines in the *Squermington Echo*, and frowned. 'You haven't lost some sort of snake, have you?'

'Not exactly.' Mrs Lind hesitated. 'George, what do you know about basilisks?'

Mostly what I knew about basilisks was that they didn't exist, except in stories. And video games. Josh had bought a game for 20p at a car boot sale. It was called *Slime Spitter:*

Battle of the Basilisks. We soon found out why it was only 20p – it kept freezing.

'Basilisks are like giant snakes. They spit slime balls at you and if you look them in the eye, they turn you into stone. You have to kill them by throwing bombs at them, or shooting them with your—'

I saw the look on Mrs Lind's face, and stopped.

'That's what I'm afraid of,' she said, quietly. 'That's what people are going to want to do to Mortifer.'

I understood now. I looked at the stone rabbit by the kitchen door. 'That's a real rabbit, isn't it?'

As Mrs Lind nodded, I remembered the stone cat Lo had brought in through the bathroom window. 'And the cat …?'

'Eleven cats. Five dogs. Eight rabbits.' Lo listed them on his fingers. 'A ridiculous number of pigeons. A fox, a badger, three squirrels and a Vietnamese pot-bellied pig. So far.'

'They're not dead,' Mrs Lind assured me. 'Just petrified. We can turn them back. That's what the ointment's for. It's my grandmother's recipe. Although I haven't quite got it to work yet.' She twisted her beads together, a worried look in her eyes. Mortifer doesn't do it on purpose, you know – he doesn't *mean* it. He can't help what he is. People never understand that. If they catch him, I can't bear to think of what will happen. It will be like Saint George and the dragon all over again.'

When both ends of the Ping Feng piglet had had enough milk, Mrs Lind put it to bed in a cardboard box.

'There's work to be done.' Lo picked up a bucket and

looked at me. 'Have you ever milked an auroch?'

I was used to getting my milk out of the fridge, not out of an animal. Especially not an animal I'd never even heard of. I shook my head.

'In that case,' said Lo, 'you had better start with Mrs Tuesday. Mrs Wednesday kicks.'

Mrs Tuesday and Mrs Wednesday turned out to be two of the giant cows, living in a paddock of their own, away from the herd. They had chocolate coats, milky noses and long, spear-like horns, and looked even bigger up close. They were much taller than I was.

Lo told me to watch while he milked Mrs Wednesday, who danced about stamping her feet and tossing her head, then he said it was my turn. He stroked Mrs Tuesday's nose and fed her peppermints while he gave me instructions.

'Be polite,' he told me, 'and she won't mind.'

I wasn't very good at it. At first the milk wouldn't come out at all, then it started going everywhere, all over the grass and my trainers.

'You'll get better,' said Lo. 'I hope.'

As we crossed the yard back to the house, we could hear the TV on in the stables.

'... Spread with chocolate fudge frosting, and decorate with sugar sprinkles . . .'

'Grissel likes cookery programmes,' said Lo. 'Especially anything to do with cake. You wouldn't guess she'd ever been a man-eater. These days, she'd rather have a muffin.'

By now, I reckoned I knew what Grissel was. What sort of animal sets fire to things and eats people? Only one that I could think of.

'So she definitely doesn't eat people?' I asked instead. I wanted to be sure on that point, before I met her.

Lo shrugged. 'Not for years. We think she may have had a bad one. The taste put her off. And she's old; she's lost a few teeth along the way. She has trouble with a pork chop, let alone human bones. But that doesn't mean she's *safe*. She's not. Especially not with people she doesn't know. It's not a good idea to go barging in on her. I'll introduce you, but not now. She was hatched in a very deep cave, and doesn't care for daylight. I take her out at night, to stretch her wings.'

Further down the row of stables, one had its doors wide open. There was sand piled thickly on the floor, and the walls were hung with mirrors.

'Mortifer's. We leave it ready, in case he comes back,' said Lo.

I remembered Josh's *Slime Spitter* game. One of the weapons you could use to kill the basilisk was a mirror. 'Aren't basilisks turned to stone by their own reflection?'

Lo shook his head. 'That's gorgons. People get them muddled up. Although it's true that basilisks don't like their reflections much. They won't look at themselves if they can help it. Those mirrors are there so you don't get taken by surprise. They're angled so you can see every corner of that stable, wherever you're standing. Like Mrs L said, Mortifer doesn't mean any harm – unless he's hungry – but you have to be careful. Look what happened to Numpty.'

'What *did* happen to him?' I wanted to know.

'He took Mortifer his dinner, forgot to check the mirrors, found himself eyeball-to-eyeball with a basilisk and turned into stone, of course,' said Lo.

I didn't want to leave, but it was getting late. Mrs Lind took money out of a cracked, blue teapot and handed it to me. I'd forgotten about getting paid. Money didn't seem important, compared with basilisks and dragons and two-headed pigs.

'Come back soon,' she told me. 'It doesn't matter when. We'll expect you when we see you.'

'And the other way round,' said Lo.

At the bottom of the track, as I was turning left into the lane, I nearly got knocked over by a bike.

My bike. And Prudence riding it.

'*You!*' I said as the bike swerved crazily and wobbled to a stop. 'You *thief*!'

For a minute, she didn't seem to know what I meant. Then she went even redder than her hair. 'Is it your bike? I didn't mean to *steal* it – not properly. I only took it because I was going to be late home. I get into trouble if I'm late. I only *borrowed* it. I mean ... I was going to give it back.'

'Oh yeah? When?'

'Today. I took it back to the Sweet Shop, where I found it. But then I saw the card: "Help Wanted. Must be the Right Person." I thought I'd get here faster if I came by bike. I didn't want to be too late.'

'You are too late,' I told her. 'Way too late. And you're the Wrong Person. I'm the Right Person. I caught the Early Mammal, and Mrs Lind gave me the job.'

You could see from Prudence's face that she minded. All she said was, 'Oh. That's that, then. I'll go ...'

'Not on my bike, you won't.' I grabbed the handlebars. 'I had to walk all the way home when you nicked it. Now it's your turn.'

Prudence slid off the saddle without arguing.

'There's a short cut through the woods,' I told her. 'See you in school.'

Unless the basilisk saw her first – and turned her into stone. She wouldn't get any sympathy from me. It would serve her right.

It felt good to be back on my bike again. Before I turned the corner, I glanced back over my shoulder. Prudence hadn't got very far. She was hanging over the fence, staring at the horse. Everyone knows that girls get soppy about ponies, so I didn't pay much attention. Which is how Prudence saw the unicorn, and I didn't.

CHAPTER SIX

iss Thripps was having one of her Whiny Wednesdays. First, she got snotty about me not handing in my homework. Then she caught me drawing in my Rough Book, when I was meant to be doing fractions.

'I've had enough of you, George Drake!' She scrunched up her mouth, so it looked like a cat's bottom, and pointed at the door. 'Head Teacher's office. Now. Go!'

The Head was on the telephone.

'You'll have to wait,' said Miss Gruff, the secretary. 'Sit down. Don't slouch, don't fidget, don't wipe your nose on the furniture, don't make a noise and don't touch anything.'

So I sat and waited. There wasn't much to do. I looked at the notices on the wall about Lost Property and Healthy Dinners and Nits. I looked at the Year 3 Ancient Egyptians Display. I looked at the Meet the Staff wall, with photos of all the teachers smiling as hard as they could, trying to look kind and cosy and as if they didn't hate children. I was so bored, I even looked in the bin. There wasn't much in it: .globs of spat-out chewing gum, a couple of snotty tissues, a pen lid and yesterday's paper. Flicking away a gum-glob, I picked up the newspaper. The Public Toilets were still closed ... A pair of stone gryphons had been stolen from outside the Squermington Towers Luxury Hotel and Health Spa ... Somebody had grown a potato that looked just like the Queen. I turned to the front page:

SQUERMINGTON WYRM EATS CHAMPION CHIHUAHUA!

Miss Elsie Spindle was waiting at the bus stop on the corner of Dandelion Drive when her prize-winning chihuahua, Cheeky Chappie Chimichanga Charlie, escaped from her handbag and ran across the road into Gardenia Gardens. Miss Spindle ran after him, very nearly getting run over by a Number 3 bus.

'I saw Charlie run into the bushes,' said Miss Spindle. 'He didn't come out again. There was something in there – I heard rustling. And there were marks in the grass, as if some gigantic thing had been slithering through it. It was that dreadful Wyrm, I know it was. It's swallowed my baby!'

A number of animals have been reported missing recently, leading to suspicions of 'pet-napping'. Is the mysterious 'pet-napper' actually the Squermington Wyrm? If so, will this ravening monster really be content with chewing on a chihuahua, or will it soon be looking for something bigger, something like a—

'Hello,' said Prudence.

I scrumpled up the newspaper and dropped it back in the bin.

'What are *you* doing here?'

'Same as you.' She flapped her Maths book at me. 'Sent out. It was harder for me. Miss Thripps kept giving me chances because I'm new.'

Under a row of neatly written fractions, Prudence had drawn a picture. Dangly earrings, pointy nose, tight little mouth like a cat's bottom. You couldn't not see who it was. Miss Thripps. Except Prudence had given her a beard. And hairy legs.

'That's not bad,' I admitted. 'What d'you want to get sent out for?'

'To talk to you.' She looked at me sideways. 'Did you tell? About the bike?'

I shook my head. I had my bike back – what was the point of making a fuss? I had more important stuff to worry about. Stuff like where an escaped basilisk might be hiding, and what did it eat, and what did it feel like being turned into stone ...?

'I haven't told. Yet,' I added, just to leave her a little bit jumpy.

Prudence scraped a blob of sticky-tack off the noticeboard and fiddled with it.

'That wasn't what I wanted to ask you ...'

'What, then?'

She turned to face me, her eyes all wide and sparkly.

'At the farm ... George, have they got *dragons*?'

It sounded silly when you said it out loud. Dragons made sense at Wormestall; not here, in the boring, ordinary real world.

'What are you on about? Why would you think that?'

'Well, there's this.' She shoved my Rough Book at me, open at the page I'd been drawing on. It was a not very good picture of Tail-biter.

'So?' I blustered. 'Josh draws spaceships all the time. It doesn't mean he's seen one. Anyway, that's not a dragon. Can't you tell? You'll be talking about *fairies* next!'

'*And*,' said Prudence, 'I saw the unicorn.'

'You *what*?'

'*And* I found this when I was walking back through the wood. I'll show you. Look ...'

She was reaching into her pocket when the door opened and there was the Head, looking down her nose at us.

'George Drake. You again,' she said, in a voice like frozen vinegar. 'And the new girl. You had better come in.'

Prudence didn't get much of a telling-off.

'I'm giving you a chance,' the Head told her, 'because you're new. And because of your Recent Sadness.' I guessed she meant the hippopotamus. 'Now go back to class. Not you, George. I haven't finished with *you*.'

By the time she *had* finished, I had a detention.

Prudence was waiting for me in the corridor.

'Well?'

'Detention.' I gave a nearby chair a kick. 'And I was going to go to Wormestall after school. I'll be late. They'll think I'm not coming.'

'I could go,' said Prudence, 'I could explain ...'

'Explain what?' I was cross with everybody, and especially her because she was nearest. 'That I'm stuck in stupid detention and you're not, and so you're a Better Person for the job? You don't fool me, with your no-mum and no-dad and your Recent Hippopotamus. You're not being *nice*. You want to steal my job, that's all. You're not just a bike thief. You're a job thief!'

'That's not fair. I didn't mean ...' began Prudence, but I wasn't listening. I ran. I legged it past the library and the lockers and the No Running in the Corridors sign, and I left her far behind. Breathless and angry, I was already back in class before I remembered the unicorn. I hadn't asked, and now I couldn't. Like it or not, I wasn't speaking to Prudence.

Miss Thripps was waffling on about it being our class's turn to do an assembly.

'As it has just been Saint George's Day,' she was saying, 'I think it would be appropriate to do something on the topic of Saint George and the dragon. A short dramatic presentation. We shall need a Narrator and a Princess and at least three people to play the dragon. And, of course, a Saint George ...'

Most of the girls stuck their hands in the air, squealing that they wanted to be the princess. Not Prudence, I noticed.

'Millie can be the Princess,' announced Miss Thripps. Millie always gets to be the princess because she can sit on her own hair.

'I'll be Saint George,' said Nathan. 'I'll kill the stupid dragon.' He was doing dragon-killing impressions with his ruler. 'I'll kill it dead. Dead. Dead. Dead.' He stabbed at Alice, who sat in front of him. 'Then I'll cut it up and put it in a pie!'

'George should be Saint George,' argued Josh. 'He's got the right name.'

Several people agreed with him. 'Yes – let George!'

'Go on, George,' said Millie, bossily. 'I don't want to be rescued by Nathan. Eeuuchh!'

'Well, George?' asked Miss Thripps. 'Do you suppose that, for once in your life, you could manage to be a saint?'

I opened my mouth, then shut it again. A week ago, I would have been pleased. I don't usually get important parts when we do plays. I end up being a Tree or Third Hedgehog or something. Now I was being offered the starring role. But did I want it?

In my mind, I could see Mrs Lind shaking her head at me. Hadn't I promised to help protect rare creatures? OK, nobody was expecting me to kill a *real* dragon, only a pretend one. Even so ...

'Couldn't we change it a bit?' I asked, not very hopefully.

'So Saint George doesn't actually *kill* the dragon? He could give it something to eat, and let it go back to its cave ...'

'Historically inaccurate!' snapped Miss Thripps. 'And a very silly idea! Buck up, George – do you want to be Saint George or not?'

'No,' I said. 'No, I don't.'

'Suit yourself!' said Miss Thripps, with a sniff. 'If you're so unwilling to join in, you can be the back end of the dragon. Not even you, George, can make a mess of that!'

Parents were invited to watch the assembly. Mum had to be at the shop and Frank had to be at school, but Harry said she'd come, as it was on her way to college.

'Will you be dressed up as a tadpole again?' she asked.

I scowled at her. Our last assembly had been on Punctuation. Miss Thripps had made me and Alice dress up as Speech Marks.

'I'm part of a dragon. The end part. Matt's the Head, Fazal's the Middle and I'm the Bum. All you'll see is my feet. So you might as well not bother.'

'I wouldn't miss it. Not for anything,' said Harry.

The dragon costume was made of cardboard boxes, a lot of green paint and an old green curtain. Matt was the only one who could actually see anything. He had a box over his head, but it had eyeholes. Fazal had to bend over, hidden by the curtain, holding onto Matt's waist, while I bent over and held on to Fazal, with the dragon's long green sausage of a tail dragging along behind me. All we could see was a patch of floor, and our feet.

Fazal said it made his back hurt.

'Stop making a fuss,' ordered Miss Thripps. 'You don't have to get into costume until it's time for you to come on. Just keep out of sight.'

We sneaked a look round the doorway as the rest of the school filed into the Hall and sat on the floor. The parents were allowed to sit in plastic chairs around the edges. I could see Harry. She'd brought popcorn and a drink, as if she was at the movies, and was texting on her mobile. Sitting quite near her was Diamond Pye, Prudence's stepmother, sucking another lollipop. Her hair wasn't pink today. It was black. She looked bored behind her mirrored sunglasses.

'I don't know why she's come,' said a voice in my ear. It was Prudence, dressed as a Village Person, with a long skirt on and a scarf tied under her chin. 'It's not as if she's my mother.'

At that moment Miss Thripps swooped down on us.

'Ssshhh!' she hissed. 'No talking! We're about to begin!'

Josh was the Narrator.

'Welcome,' he said loudly, 'to 6T's assembly. I hope you find it interesting.'

It wasn't that interesting – not until St George nearly poked out one of the Village People's eyeballs with his plastic sword. The Village Person began to cry, all blinky and runny-nosed. Then St George knocked off the Princess's jewelled crown.

'Oi! Watch what you're doing, Nathan, you thicko!' said Millie, in a not-at-all-princessy voice.

Behind me I heard Miss Thripps let out a groan.

'Quickly, boys!' She started shoving Fazal and me under our curtain. 'Get out there. At least he's *supposed* to kill *you*!'

Nathan certainly did his best to kill us. He slashed and whacked and jabbed at us. Matt was blundering about in the dark because his cardboard head had been bashed sideways and he'd lost his eyeholes. He tripped over his own feet, and died before he was meant to. Fazal, holding on to him, went over too. I let go of Fazal, just in time, but held on to my share of the curtain. Nathan stabbed me. It hurt. Annoyed, I kicked him. He yelled, which was nice, so I kicked him again and he fell over.

Year 3, sitting cross-legged nearest the action, were in an uproar.

'The Dragon's Bum's killing Saint George!' they squealed. 'Yay! Fight! Fight!'

The stuffy darkness had lightened. Nathan's slashing and slicing had ripped the curtain. If I tweaked the material until the hole reached one of my eyes, I could see. I could see the parents, looking politely puzzled. I could see Harry, grinning and taking photos on her mobile. I could see the Head, clearing her throat and rising to her feet. I could even see all the way to the back of the Hall, where the big arched windows looked out onto the playground – where, slithering in between the climbing frame and the slide, I could see the tail end of something huge and scaly ...

Mortifer.

Nobody else had seen. The audience had their backs to the window, and all the actors were watching Nathan flail around on the floor. Everyone except Prudence. She was staring out at the playground, her eyes wide and bright with excitement.

Any minute now, the Head was going to do her 'Thank-you-for-coming-now-please-go-away' speech. All the parents would stand up and turn round and look out of the window and then there would be a massive fuss. The police would come, and say that Mortifer was a dangerous animal. Maybe they'd be right, but he was Mrs Lind's dangerous animal and she wanted him back.

'Nathan! Stand up and kill the rest of that dragon!' hissed Miss Thripps. 'George! For goodness' sake, lie down and die! Narrator! Get on with it!'

'Um, right ...' said Josh. 'So the dragon was dead – most of it, anyway – and George became a saint.' Everyone looked at Nathan, who was still rolling around, clutching his knee. I hadn't even kicked him that hard. I was only wearing socks. 'And everybody lived happily ever after because there were no more dragons. The End.'

'Well, that was all very interesting,' said the Head in a hurry. 'A very *lively* performance, I'm sure we all agree. And now, if the parents would like to make their way out ...'

Mothers shuffled on their seats, picking up their handbags. Fathers packed away their cameras. I glanced out of the window. The tip of a tail was still visible. There was a Green Area next to the playground. There wasn't much in it – a pond full of weeds, a broken swing and some bushes – but there were places for a basilisk to hide. If I could just keep everyone sitting down for a few more minutes ...

'Maybe Saint George killed *that* dragon,' I said, as loudly and clearly as I could through a mouthful of curtain. 'But it wasn't the only one. What about the Squermington Wyrm?'

That did it. All eyes turned my way.

'The Wyrm's not real. It's just a stupid story!' called out a boy in Year 5. 'My dad says so.'

'Your dad's wrong,' I told him. 'The Wyrm's just as real as you are.'

'How do you know?' taunted another Year 5.

Struggling out of my curtain, I took a deep breath.

'Because I've seen it,' I said.

There was a moment's silence, then one of the smallest Year 3s started to cry. A movement caught the corner of my eye: Prudence, frantically shaking her head at me. She looked scared. I wondered why. It wasn't the basilisk that had upset her, so what was it? She ducked her head, glancing away from me towards the audience. A lot of people were smiling: they didn't believe me. Others were looking shocked, or worried: they weren't quite sure. And then there was Prudence's stepmother.

Diamond Pye wasn't smiling – and she had stopped looking bored. She had taken her sunglasses off her nose and her lollipop out of her mouth. She was leaning forward in her seat, her eyes drilling into mine as if she was trying to see right through my eyeballs and inside my mind.

Miss Thripps said I was a disruptive element and an attention-seeker.

'Don't think you can get away with it,' she huffed. 'Just because you come from a broken home.'

I didn't know what she meant at first. The only thing that was broken at home was the washing machine. Then I realized she was talking about Dad.

'We're not *broken*,' I said. 'We still work. We've just got a bit missing.'

Miss Thripps squished up her lips and told me to go back to the classroom. I was on my way out of the Hall when fingers closed round my wrist. Long black fingernails dug into my skin.

'Hello, boy,' said Diamond Pye.

It's rude to stare. But sometimes it's very difficult not to. Diamond was all in black. Tight black trousers. Black shirt. Long black hair piled up on top of her head. Even her lollipop was black. Only her high-heeled boots were silver. Hanging on a silver chain from her neck was the head of a small black bird. It looked as if it was dripping blood, but the drops were actually crimson crystals, glowing against Diamond's skin. The bird's feet hung from her ears, its little crooked claws brushing her neck.

'You've seen the Wyrm.' She licked her lips. '*Where is it?*'

I shook my head, trying to pull my hand free. 'I don't

know.' Which was true. I glanced out of the window: there was no sign of Mortifer.

But Mortifer could not be far away. And I didn't think that anybody who wore bits of dead bird in their ears was a proper person to find him.

'The Wyrm's a made-up story. Nobody believes it. Not really.'

Diamond's grip tightened on my arm. 'You said you'd seen it!'

I shrugged. 'Only joking – ouch!'

Her nails were stabbing my flesh. 'Joking? Why would you do that?'

For once, Miss Thripps came in useful.

'I'm a Disruptive Attention-Seeker,' I said, firmly. 'From a Broken Home.'

Diamond laughed her tinkly wind-chime laugh, and let me go.

'When Prudence lies,' she told me, softly, 'I always know. And I teach her a lesson. Children need to be taught lessons. It's good for them. Run along, boy. Run away. I don't need you. My men are out there, looking for the Wyrm. They'll find it soon enough. And when they've found it, do you know what I'm going to do?'

I shook my head. Diamond gave her lollipop a delicate little lick and smiled a crocodile smile.

'I shall catch it. And bag it. And stuff it.'

CHAPTER SEVEN

I hadn't been back to Wormestall all week. When Mum heard about my detention, she grounded me. Miss Thripps must have said something to her about broken homes.

'I'm not having you running wild,' she told me, knotting one of her legs around the other one. 'Just because your father's not here.'

'I've got a job,' I pointed out. 'That's not the same thing as running wild. They'll be expecting me.' I couldn't even ring, because of Wormestall having no phone. 'I can't just not turn up for a whole week. It's ... it's unprofessional.'

'Getting detention's unprofessional!' snapped Mum, hanging onto the fridge to stop herself falling over. 'You should have thought of that earlier!'

I could only hope that Mrs Lind hadn't got tired of waiting for me, and given my job away to anyone else. Anyone like Prudence.

As I turned up the track to Wormestall, a van shot past me. It had been dawdling behind my bike since I came off the main road, although I'd given it plenty of room to overtake. An ordinary black van – except I was sure I had seen it before, parked on our road. It had been there when I left home, a few doors down from my house. The two men inside had both been holding up newspapers, so I had not seen their faces. I didn't see them now, either, but I wasn't really looking. I had other things on my mind.

Halfway up the track, I leant my bike against the fence and looked for the horse.

He was over in the far corner of the field: a black mountain of a shire horse, with a white blaze and shaggy socks, hoofs the size of dinner plates, and a tangled tail. He must have sensed me staring because, after a minute or two, he took his nose out of the hedge, turned round and blew a loud raspberry at me.

I should have known. This was Wormestall after all.

It didn't look like any of the pictures I've ever seen of unicorns: prancing, dancing things, with floaty manes and pearly horns. But – grass stained and muddy, covered in bits of bramble leaf and about as long as my arm – that was definitely a horn.

The unicorn trotted up to the fence and whickered at me. I patted his neck. The skin twitched beneath my hand, but he didn't seem to mind. I stroked his nose while he lipped at my T-shirt. It wasn't until I reached out to touch his horn that he tossed his head and cantered away from me. I tried calling him back but unicorns don't come when they're called, so I got back on my bike and pedalled up to the house.

The door was open but there wasn't a note on it this time, so, to be polite, I clanged the bell.

'Must you make that racket?' said a voice. 'Can't you see the door's open?'

It was Lo. As I stepped into the hall, he was coming down the stairs, his arms full of sheets and towels.

'I'm sorry I'm late. It's not my fault,' I said, in a rush. 'I had detention and Mum grounded me and I've seen Mortifer, he came to my school and ... What's that?'

I'd trodden in something. Something wet and sticky. There was a trail of it leading to the kitchen door. It looked a lot like—

'Blood,' said Lo.

In the kitchen, Dido was sitting on her egg collection. She glared at us and clicked her beak, but in a half-hearted sort of way.

There were puddles of blood everywhere. In the middle of it all, at the kitchen table, sat Mrs Lind, pressing a red-stained towel against her arm.

'Hello, George. I knew you'd come!' Her voice was cheerful, but her face was ghostly-pale.

I stared. 'What happened?'

In answer, she lifted the cloth a few centimetres away from her skin. More blood splashed on to the floor. She covered the wound again, but not before I had seen the jagged tear in her flesh, and the gleam of bone.

And the teeth marks.

'*What* did *that*?'

'There's something new in the duck pond.' Lo was ripping up a sheet.

'It wasn't there yesterday,' said Mrs Lind. 'I went to feed the fish, but there weren't any left ... It must have been very hungry, poor thing. There was a drowning bee. I put my hand in the water to rescue it and ... snap!'

'You – Saint George – put the kettle on,' Lo ordered me. 'We want hot water. And this.' Pulling the first aid box down from the dresser, he took out a little bottle full of what looked like sugar crystals.

I squinted at the spidery writing on the label: '*Alicorn ~ Use with care*'.

'She needs stitches.' Even I could see that. 'She needs to go to hospital.' I didn't know how we were going to get her there. With no phone, we couldn't even ring for an ambulance.

'Hospital? What for?' Lo had pulled down a second box. This one was marked 'Sewing'. Inside were all the things you would expect – a rainbow of cotton reels, pincushion, scissors, thimbles ... and needles.

I stared at him. Was he planning to sew her up like an old pair of trousers?

'You can't! That's not how they do it!

They have special needles and special thread and ... and stuff.'

And doctors and nurses and people who know what they're doing.

'No hospital. No doctors,' said Lo. 'They ask too many questions. Now get a move on, before she runs out of blood.'

I looked at Mrs Lind. She was the colour of skimmed milk. I gave in, and picked up the kettle.

Lo was choosing a needle.

'You should sterilize that,' I said. I knew this, from the time Harry decided to pierce her own ear. The germs got in, and she went around dribbling pus for days.

'Don't need to,' said Lo. He took the top off the alicorn bottle, sprinkling it over the wound as if he was salting chips. 'No germs stand a chance against this stuff.'

'What is it?' I asked.

'Powdered unicorn horn,' said Lo, licking the crystals off his fingers.

'Oh,' I said. 'And you get it from ...?'

'Big Nigel.' Lo nodded. 'Although it's a bit of a struggle. He's not that keen on having his horn grated.'

I was all right until Lo picked up the needle. It flashed silver between his fingers, then swooped. The room began to swim and blur, pinpricks of light dancing before my eyes. A wave of sickness washed through me.

'I think ...' I heard myself say. 'I think I might have to sit down ...'

I'm fine with blood. I'm not so good with needles.

I heard an impatient sound from Lo, then a voice saying urgently, 'He's going to fall. Get a chair ...'

There was the scrape of wood across flagstones and somebody gave me a shove. My knees folded, and I crumpled backwards into the open arms of the rocking chair.

'Sorry,' I mumbled. 'It's just ... needles. I'll be OK in a minute. Carry on without me.'

I did feel better after a few minutes of sitting with my eyes closed, breathing in the smell of disinfectant. Better, and embarrassed. I stood up.

'Er – sorry. I'm fine now. Can I help?'

Lo was a fast worker. The wound was nearly closed, with a row of impressively neat stitches.

'You can try not doing that again, for a start. I told you before – this is no place to be squeamish.'

'Don't be unkind, Lo.' Mrs Lind smiled at me. 'George isn't used to us yet – and the way we do things.'

'He had better *get* used to it,' said Lo. 'And quickly. There's no point hanging around – you'll just be in the way,' he told me. 'If you want to make yourself useful, you can go and feed the ducks.'

I was relieved. I used to feed the ducks on the river with my gran, when I was a little kid. You just chuck bread at them. Easy.

'They'll be hungry. They'll come running,' said Mrs Lind. 'Just give them a call – Donald and Jemima – then throw the food down for them. They won't bother you.'

'Food's in a bucket by the back door,' said Lo, head bent over his stitching.

'No problem,' I said, cheerfully. 'And where are the ducks?'

'Where d'you think? Try the duck pond. Through the vegetable patch into the orchard, then turn right, down the hill. You can't miss it.'

'The pond? Isn't that where ...?' I looked at Mrs Lind's arm. She'd been lucky not to get her whole hand bitten off. What lived in a duck pond and did *that* to people?

'It's all right,' she promised me. 'It had flippers and a fin – some sort of ichthyosaur, I think. It won't leave the water. It's muddy down there. You can borrow a pair of wellingtons.'

'Just remember,' said Lo, tweaking a stitch tight. 'If you go for a paddle, I'm not sewing your feet back on.'

There were two buckets waiting outside the door. One contained slabs of glistening raw meat, buzzing with flies and reminding me unpleasantly of the inside of Mrs Lind's arm. The other was full of crumbled bread crusts. Not rocket science to work out which was meant for the ducks.

I walked through the vegetable garden and on past the orchard, full of fruit trees and bees and wild flowers in the long grass, then turned right. The borrowed boots were too big. My feet slid around inside them, which made walking uncomfortable, but it didn't matter because there, ahead of me, was the duck pond.

'Donald! Jemima!' I called, swinging my bucket.

They'll be hungry. They'll come running.

Why hadn't I heard the warning? Probably because – call me stupid – I had been expecting something duck-sized. Something that waddled and quacked.

'Donald,' I called again. 'JemimaAAAAAGH!'

The 'ducks' had burst out from behind a clump of trees. Taller than grown men, they looked like a cross between an ostrich and a velociraptor, with glossy feathers and gigantic, curved beaks, specially designed to rip me to pieces and crunch up my bones. They didn't quack – they honked. And they didn't waddle – they *galumphed* on bright yellow feet the size of pizzas.

Pulling myself together, I hurled the contents of the bucket as far away from me as possible. Honking greedily, Donald and Jemima braked, flapping wings that didn't look big enough for their massive bodies, and lowered their heads to inspect their breakfast.

They poked the bread with their beaks, turning it upside down, as if there might be something hiding underneath. Then they flung it about a bit. After that they lost interest in it. Raising their heads, stretching out their long necks, they focused on me.

My stomach lurched. *I had brought the wrong bucket.* These birds didn't eat bread. Not with those beaks. No, Donald and Jemima liked raw meat.

And the only raw meat on the horizon was me.

I could hear the mutterings at school, in assembly, in the

corridors, in the changing rooms: *'Heard about George Drake? Yeah, eaten by a duck ...'*

Donald and Jemima had separated, stalking towards me from different directions. *They're hunting you.* My heart was thudding. *They're working as a team: you haven't got a chance ...*

I wasn't ready to be a ducks' dinner. I looked around me. What choices did I have? The birds were cutting off my line of escape to the farmhouse. I didn't think I could outrun them, anyway – they had legs like rugby players. In front of me lay the still waters of the pond, which was actually more of a small lake. I thought of what had happened to Mrs Lind's arm, and shuddered. *No, not the pond.* I looked at the clump of trees growing by the water's edge. I was pretty sure Donald and Jemima couldn't fly: those stumpy wings would never get them off the ground. I, on the other hand, am not bad at climbing.

The only way was up.

I made a dash for the nearest tree, grabbed hold of a branch and swung myself clear of the ground. Just in time. Lighter and faster than Donald, Jemima had put on a burst of speed. As I swung out of reach, she made a lunge and caught my leg in her crushing machine of a beak. Desperately, I tried yanking my foot free. To my surprise, it came. Jemima was left with a green boot sticking out of her beak. I didn't like to think what would have happened if it had been a tighter fit.

While Jemima was busy ripping the wellie into little

shreds of green rubber, Donald arrived at the foot of the tree, stamping his flat pizza feet and doing his best to reach me by snaking out his neck and snapping his big red beak.

The snaps were missing my feet by millimetres. I needed to climb higher, but it was the wrong sort of tree. The upper branches were too narrow and twiggy; they wouldn't take my weight. Instead, all I could do was scramble to the far end of one of the lower branches, overhanging the water.

I was out of Donald's reach, but I wasn't feeling at all happy. I remembered Dolphin Park. The dolphins had exploded out of the water, to loop the loop and leap through hoops. They were very good at it, even the mighty killer whale. They had jumped easily as high as my branch. I could only hope that ichthyosaurs weren't that acrobatic. I sat gripping my branch, staring into the depths below me and wondering if that was a dark shape I could see, stirring in the pond weed, or just a shadow.

Donald got bored of snapping at thin air, and had another idea. He seized one of the lower branches in his beak and began shaking his head from side to side. The whole tree rocked, nearly tipping me into the water. It was then that I heard the first crack.

No. Please. Not.

Another vigorous head shake from Donald. Another crack.

No-please no-please no-pleasepleaseplease ...

Suddenly, the smooth surface of the water broke beneath me, and something sleek and silvery rose up out of it, like in the stories of King Arthur's sword. Except that this looked more like a chainsaw than a sword. I had never seen so many teeth in one mouth before. Even the ducks backed off, honking in alarm.

Heart slamming against my ribs, I wrapped my legs around my dying branch. Any minute now there would be a final crack and I would be in the pond with the ichthyosaur.

I'd never really thought about dying, not properly. Mum was going to be upset. She'd have to do a lot of yoga before she cheered up again. And she'd have to email Dad. Would he come home for my funeral? Would there be enough of me left to *have* a funeral? Harry would burst into tears. Harry's always bursting into tears, but it never lasts very long. Frank cried for a day and a half when her hamster died, but that was a hamster. I was just her brother. Would she wish she had been nicer to me? Or would she just want the 83p redundancy money back ...?

CRACK!

I was in the water.

When Mum told Dad she hoped he got eaten by a shark, I did some research. He wasn't going to be winning Dad of the Year Award any time soon; that didn't mean he deserved to be fish food. I sent him an email, with instructions on How Not To Get Eaten. He emailed me back: Cheers, mate. You've been watching too many Jaws movies! Love, Dad xox. Which wasn't very grateful of him, seeing how long I'd spent on the Internet when I was supposed to be doing my Maths homework.

It's much more difficult remembering the Top Tips on How Not To Get Eaten when you're about to get eaten.

Don't panic. When you've just fallen into a pond inhabited by a hungry prehistoric monster, this is very helpful advice. Not.

Don't splash. This will attract the predator. A bit late for that. I had already made a massive splash, dive-bombing out of the tree.

Don't bleed. Predators can smell your blood from up to five kilometres away. Failed again. I had grazed my hand on a rough branch.

Punch the predator in the eyes. This thing's jaw was longer than my arm. I'd never get anywhere near its eyes.

Shout loudly, to distract the predator and gain the attention of rescuers. My mouth was full of pond water, and my throat seemed to have closed up. I tried shouting. It came out as a sort of bubbly gurgle.

Get out of the water. Well, DUH! I could have thought of that one for myself, thank you.

I was out of my depth, tangled in weed, and my one remaining wellington, now full of water, was weighing me down. Gasping with cold, I swam as fast – and unsplashily – as I could to the edge of the pond. The bank was steep, here, and very crumbly. I scrabbled at it, trying to get a grip, but it was like trying to climb a wall of damp sand.

Treading water, I looked over my shoulder. The surface

of the water was as smooth as glass. Where was it?

Then something bumped against my leg.

My mouth and throat dry with fear, I stared down into the depths.

Where? *Where?*

There – beneath me, a sleek, grey shape, weaving through the weed.

Ignoring the No Splashing rule, I kicked out savagely. If I was really lucky, I might get it in the eye after all.

The kick took my wellington off. I felt it go. There was a sudden thrashing and boiling of water and that chainsaw jaw broke the surface. Speared between those terrible teeth was my boot.

My very own Top Tip on How Not To Get Eaten: wear wellington boots. They can buy you time.

Ripples fanned out behind the ichthyosaur as it headed back into the centre of the pond with its trophy. I didn't have very long. It would soon lose interest in a rubber boot.

I dug my fingers into the earth. Above my head, just out of reach, a tree root poked out. If I could get hold of that, I'd be able to heave myself up ... I stretched up for it, stretching until my shoulder ached. *Please, please, please ... I'll be good for the rest of my life, really I will. I'll do my homework ...* My fingertips were a hair's breadth away from the root, but it was no use. I was doomed.

I glanced back over my shoulder, just in time to see an angry tail slap the water. The water rippled, and this time the arrow was pointing straight at me. It was coming fast, coming in for the kill. I shut my eyes and started to count. The last time I'd ever play the Million Game – and I'd be lucky if I even got to ten …

Then two things happened at once. Something fell into the water with a splash, and somebody said my name.

'George. Give me your hand. Now.'

I opened my eyes. Lo was kneeling on the bank, holding out his hand. I raised my arm; he gripped my wrist and pulled. He was stronger than he looked. I slithered up that bank and flopped on the grass like a landed trout.

I lay on my back, full of relief and pond water, listening to the drumming of my heart. Lo reached into the plastic bucket beside him and chucked a second lump of meat into the pond. I turned my head in time to see the chainsaw rise up and snatch it before it hit the water.

'Good catch!' approved Lo. 'You don't see many ichthyosaurs around. Not for the last ninety million years or so.'

I turned my head the other way. Donald and Jemima were happily ripping bits of cow apart.

'Ducks,' I said, bitterly. '*Ducks*, you said.'

Lo grinned. '*Bullockornis*. Demon Ducks of Doom. Fifteen million years out of date, but they don't care! After you'd gone, Mrs L remembered she'd left two buckets out – the one you took was for the pig. We thought you might be having a spot of bother. They're not very keen on bread. Wrong sort of duck.'

My legs felt like jelly. When I stood up, I found I was

limping. Jemima's attack on my boot had bruised my ankle. One good thing about thinking you're about to die: you don't care about little things like a sore foot.

Donald and Jemima, to my relief, had disappeared back into the trees. All that was left of their Meat Feast was a patch of bloodstained grass.

'You'll know next time,' said Lo, picking up crusts of bread and dropping them back into the bucket.

'I'm not likely to forget,' I agreed. 'Demon Ducks of Doom don't eat bread.'

As we crossed the yard, the television blared out from the stables.

'Grissel's been chewing the remote again,' said Lo. 'She keeps turning up the volume.'

In the kitchen, Mrs Lind was asleep in the rocking chair with her arm in a sling made out of a towel. The Early Mammal was eating sweetcorn on her hat and the Ping Feng piglet was curled up in her lap.

'Mandrake and lettuce juice,' said Lo, pointing at an empty glass on the table. 'It knocks you right out. She won't wake up for hours.' He looked me up and down. 'You've got pondweed in your hair. I suppose you'd better have some dry clothes.'

He took me upstairs to a room with splintery floorboards and a bare mattress. Rummaging in a wooden chest, he threw me a T-shirt with a flaming motorbike and the words 'Live Fast' on it. When I held it up, several black feathers floated to the floor.

'It's ripped,' I said. It had a long tear in both shoulders.

'Take it or leave it,' said Lo.

'Is this your bedroom?' I asked. My bedroom's painted blue, with Batman curtains and posters of footballers on the walls.

'What would I do with a bedroom?' He tossed me a pair of black jeans. 'I'll leave you to change. Come down when you're ready.'

There was something uncomfortable about that room, with its drifting feathers and spidery corners. The jeans were too long. I stayed just long enough to roll them up, then hurried downstairs.

CHAPTER EIGHT

There was no sign of Lo in the kitchen. Mrs Lind was still asleep. I didn't want to wake her, and I wasn't keen on being left alone with Dido, who was back on her eggs, fluffing up her feathers and clicking her beak at me, so I took my wet clothes outside, to dry in the sun. If it hadn't been for Grissel turning up the TV, I would have heard the sound of the engine sooner.

I was draping my *All Star Zombie Smackdown* T-shirt over the open door to Mortifer's stable when the van came round the corner of the house and bumped to a stop on the cobblestones. The same black van that had been following me earlier. My skin began prickling, the way it does when you know something's wrong but you're not sure what.

The passenger door opened and a man got out. The first thing you noticed about him was how tidy he was. He was wearing a lilac waistcoat and a lilac spotted bow-tie. His black hair was so neat, it looked as if it had been painted onto his head, and he had one of those pointy little beards that look better on a goat. The next thing you noticed was that one of his hands wasn't there. Instead, he had a hook, like a pantomime pirate.

The driver had a bit of trouble squeezing himself out of his seat. He was more of a giant baby than a man, with a bald head and rolls of fat where his neck should have been. His face was shiny with sweat, and he looked as if he might burst out of his suit at any minute.

The neat little man stared very hard at me, then gave me a neat little smile.

'Good afternoon, young man. We're from the Council. We just need to take a quick look around.' His eyes were on the stables. 'That's all right, isn't it?'

I shook my head. 'Not really, no,' I said. 'You'll have to talk to Mrs Lind, and you can't because she's asl— because you can't.'

'Actually, we can do what we like.' He flashed a small square of plastic at me, too quickly for me to read what was written on it.

'We're from Dad,' he said.

'Whose dad?' I didn't trust him. 'Not mine. He's in Australia.'

'D-A-D.' Goatbeard made it sound very important. 'Dangerous Animals Department. There have been reports of an unexplained Large Reptile. In the interests of Public Health and Safety, it is our duty to check all outbuildings.'

'Do you have a search warrant?' I asked. They ask that a lot on TV.

'Oh, it's hardly a matter for the police,' said Goatbeard, running his fingers along his hook. 'As long as people co-operate. Have you *seen* any Dangerous Animals recently, young man?'

I shook my head. Goatbeard raised his eyebrows, as if he didn't believe me.

'There's nothing here,' I said. 'The last I heard, the Squermington Wyrm was right over the other side of town.'

That bit was true. After our assembly, Mortifer had disappeared from the school grounds without anyone spotting him. There had been another sighting of him reported in the news this morning. Somebody driving to High Upton after dark had had to brake and wait while something 'as thick as a tree trunk' crossed the road in front of him.

'We know about that,' said Goatbeard. 'We're searching everywhere. But we're starting here. Stand aside. I want to see inside that stable.'

I shrugged, and moved out of the way. There was nothing to interest them in Mortifer's empty stable, and I needed time to work out how to keep them away from Grissel. She might have swapped eating people for cupcakes and the Cookery Channel, but I was pretty sure she still counted as a Dangerous Animal.

'Nothing there,' said Goatbeard, after a quick look inside. He stopped to admire his reflection, smoothing his hair and tweaking his bow tie. 'Peculiar place to hang a lot of mirrors, isn't it?'

'Mrs Lind likes to know her hat's on straight,' I told him.

Goatbeard gave me a suspicious look. 'Open the next one!' he ordered Giant Baby.

'Unnghh,' said Giant Baby, obediently.

I had the beginnings of a plan. Whether it worked rather depended on what was in that stable. I didn't know, any more than they did. This was Wormestall, so it could be anything – from Bigfoot to a sabre-tooth tiger.

'What the blazes ...?' Whatever Goatbeard had been expecting, it wasn't this.

Stone animals, piled up on top of each other, all with labels around their necks. Rabbits, squirrels, dogs, cats. There was Charlie the champion chihuahua, and the Vietnamese pot-bellied pig, right at the back. Two of the statues puzzled me a bit. The size of a large dog, they looked like eagles from the front and lions from the back. Then I remembered the newspaper report about the missing gryphons, stolen from outside the Squermington Towers Hotel.

'What's all this about?' Goatbeard was inside the stable, poking around among the animals.

'Nnnghh.' Giant Baby lumbered in after him, bending down to stroke a stone cat.

They were both in my trap. I slammed the doors shut behind them, dragging the bolts across as quickly as I could.

'You little toad!' snarled Goatbeard's voice. 'You wait until I get out of here! I'll skin you alive!'

My heart beating hard and fast, I listened to the curses coming from inside.

'You'll be sorry when she hears about this!' spat Goatbeard.

I was wondering who *she* was when, out of the corner of my eye, I noticed something.

The door to Grissel's stable was swinging open – and *something* was on its way out.

Something with two legs and a lot of red hair.

'*You!*' I said. 'What are *you* doing here?'

Putting her finger to her lips, Prudence grabbed me by the arm and dragged me away from the stable door, out of earshot.

'You have to get rid of them,' she hissed.

'I'm trying!' I hissed back. 'It's not as easy as all that. They're from the Council. From the Dangerous Animals Department.'

Prudence shook her head, violently. 'No, they're not. They're not from the department of anything. They're Mr Mintzer and Mr Mump, and they work for my stepmother. They've been following you ever since you opened your big mouth in assembly and told everyone you'd seen the Wyrm!'

'I did see it! It was there, outside the window. And I only said that to stop everybody turning round and seeing it for themselves. It only got away because of me!'

'Whatever,' said Prudence. 'The point

is – now they're after you. I came to warn you.'

I looked towards Grissel's stable.

'How long have you been in there?'

'I stopped to talk to the unicorn – I brought him some carrots. I'd just come up to the house when I heard the van turn onto the track. I knew it was them. I had to hide.'

The left side of her face, now I looked at her properly, was bright pink, and she smelled quite strongly of singed hair. Her fringe had gone frizzy.

'Are you all right ...?'

'It got quite hot in there,' admitted Prudence. 'She set fire to my hair, actually, but there was a bucket of water, so I just stuck my head in it. It sizzled a bit. Then we both had a doughnut and it was OK after that. We watched *Will You Win a Million?*'

I stared at her. 'You shut yourself in with a dragon, and you ate *doughnuts* and watched a *game show* with her?'

Prudence was licking sugar off her fingers. 'She likes doughnuts. I brought a bag with me – it's a long walk. I was going to give you one, but I'm afraid they're all gone. Don't look at me like that. There are some things much scarier than dragons, you know. Some people—'

She broke off, as something crashed against the inside of the stable door.

Prudence flinched. 'They're getting out! George – you have to make them go away. Tell Mr Mintzer – he's the one with the hook – tell him you know who he is. If that doesn't work, tell him you know what he did.'

'What did he do?'

Another crash, then another, shook the door on its hinges.

Prudence was trembling. 'I'll explain later. Tell him you know what happened at the zoo – that you know about Long Sally.'

'Long *who*?'

Crash! Goatbeard's metal hook flashed, slashing at the timber. Prudence gave a squeak of fear, and disappeared back in with Grissel.

Goatbeard and Giant Baby came bursting out. Goatbeard was frothing at the mouth with fury. He shook his hook at me, ready to lunge.

'Do you know what this is, boy? It's a snake hook. Do you know what's it for? Dealing with poisonous wigglers – like you!'

I took a deep breath and hoped very much that Prudence knew what she was talking about.

'You're not from the Council,' I told him. 'Your name is Mr Mintzer and I know what happened at the zoo.'

It worked. Mr Mintzer lowered his hook.

'I don't believe you,' he growled. '*What* do you know?'

'I know about Long Sally,' I said. 'And if you don't leave – right now – I shall tell the police.'

He glared at me. He had the sort of small eyes that look quite nice on a pig. On him, they just looked mean.

'A clever little know-it-all, aren't you?' he sneered. 'Very well, we're leaving. And you're coming with us!'

'No!' I took a step backwards, but the silver hook flashed out and caught me by the elbow.

'You can tell Mrs Pye everything you know. And when you've finished,' said Mr Mintzer, 'we'll feed you to the Squermington Wyrm. Just as soon as we've found it – and that won't take us long. Open up the van, Mr Mump. We'll put him in the back. He'll be less trouble.'

But Mr Mump's baby face had suddenly frozen, his eyes bulging.

'Nnnghh!' he said. 'Moo!'

'What are you mooing about, you great loaf!' snapped Mintzer.

'Nnnghh!' said Mr Mump again, pointing at something behind us.

Oh no! I thought, feeling suddenly icy cold. *Not Grissel!* Surely Prudence hadn't let her out? I looked down at Mintzer's gleaming hook, and my fingers curled into fists. I wasn't going to let that hook anywhere near Grissel, or Mortifer, or any of the other animals at Wormestall – not if I could help it.

Mintzer had let go of my arm, and was staring in the same direction as Mump. I turned round.

It wasn't Grissel. It was Lo – and Mrs Wednesday.

'People,' said Lo. His eyes had narrowed to turquoise slits, and his black hair seemed spikier than usual. 'We don't like people much.' He looked at me. 'Why are they here?'

'They're impostors.' I told him. 'They said they were from the Dangerous Animals Department, but they're not. They lied.'

'That's a pity,' said Lo. 'We especially don't like liars.'

He led Mrs Wednesday forward by her rope halter, until her long, sharp-tipped horns scratched the paint on the side of the van. Mr Mintzer was caught between them. I saw him gulp.

'Stay away from me, boy!' His voice came out a bit higher than usual. 'Or you'll be sorry!'

'Will I? Are you sure?' asked Lo. 'One of us is holding a very large animal. And it isn't you. We're late with the milking today. That always puts her in a bad mood. Did you know, you are twenty-seven times more likely to get killed by a cow than you are by a shark? Right now, in your case, I would say it was more like a hundred and twenty-seven times ...'

Mr Mintzer gave him a nasty look. 'Start the van, Mump,' he said, ducking under Mrs Wednesday's horns. 'We're leaving.'

'What did they want?' Lo demanded, when the sound of the van's engine had faded away. 'Who were they?'

'You'd better ask Prudence.' I told him. She's in the stables. With Grissel.'

Lo frowned. 'What?'

I shrugged. 'I didn't bring her here. She came by herself. She found Grissel and they've been eating doughnuts and watching TV together. If you don't believe me, go and see.'

Lo shut Mrs Wednesday in an empty stable,

then took me by the arm. His grip was as fierce as Mr Mintzer's hook.

'You can come with me,' he said, grimly. 'And if your friend's really in there, you had better hope Grissel hasn't cooked her to a crisp.'

I started to say that Prudence was not my friend, then I stopped. It didn't really matter. What mattered was that, at last, I was going to meet Grissel.

The nearest thing to meeting your first proper dragon is that feeling you get when you're waiting to dive off something really high, or ride on the biggest roller-coaster ever. A sort of knot inside your stomach that leaves you part-scared, part-excited, part-happy and part-a-tiny- bit-sick.

Several stables had been knocked into one to make room for Grissel, the walls charred and blackened with soot. From nose to tail tip, she would have stretched the length of a train carriage, with a bit left over. Now she lay curled on a pile of smooth stones, with the end of her tail draped over her nose, her eyes fixed on an old portable TV.

You could tell she was ancient. Her coppery scales were tarnished and dull, as if she had been left out in the rain for about a hundred years. One wing stuck out at an angle, like a broken umbrella spoke, and there was a dent in her side where the scales grew all crooked. Her one eye was clouded, milky with cataract. Where the other eye should have been, there was a puckered nothing. She was old and battered, but you could still sense her power. A smoky haze of danger hung in the air, smelling faintly of gunpowder and barbecued sausages. I stood in the doorway, in no great hurry to go any further.

'What happened to her eye?' I whispered to Lo.

'Your Saint George. He stuck a spear in it, didn't he? He left her for dead. But he wasn't quite as clever as he thought he was. She dragged herself into hiding, before the villagers arrived with their pitchforks to finish her off.'

I thought of the iron point piercing the jelly of the eyeball. And twisting. I winced.

'He's not *my* Saint George. He's nothing to do with me.' I frowned. 'You don't mean she's Saint George's *actual* dragon? But all that – that was ages ago.'

'Seventeen hundred years, give or take a few. Nothing special, for a dragon.'

Awed, I gazed at Grissel. She paid no attention. She was concentrating on a programme about cheesecake.

'What happened to her wing? Was that Saint George, too?'

'No. That was broken much later. In the War.'

'What was she doing in the War?'

'Minding her own business,' snapped Lo. 'Like most people who get hurt in your stupid wars. She was flying at night; somebody thought she was an enemy plane and an anti-aircraft gun ripped right through her wing. She's been through a lot of history. Enough to put her off humans.'

All except Prudence, apparently.

Prudence was sitting near the pile of stones, hugging her

knees.

'She saw the advertisement for the job,' I told Lo. 'And she knows about the unicorn.'

Lo raised his eyebrows. 'In that case,' he said, 'Mrs Lind will want to meet her. She had better come in.'

In the kitchen, Mrs Lind was just waking up.

'Today is full of surprises,' she said, blinking at Prudence. 'First an ichthyosaur, now a girl ...'

You could see Prudence was nervous, but her eyes lit up as she took in Dido in the dog basket and the two-headed piglet on Mrs Lind's lap. Mrs Lind's hat lay on the kitchen table, covered in its usual litter of half-eaten fruit.

'What a lovely hat,' said Prudence, politely.

She put out a hand to touch the band of fur stretched around the brim, then snatched it back, blood oozing from her finger.

Serves her right, I thought, *for sucking up*!

Lo laughed. 'You like the hat, but the hat doesn't like you!'

Mrs Lind tut-tutted at the Early Mammal who was chittering angrily, disturbed from his nap.

'Naughty Mingus.' Then she noticed Prudence's pink cheek and frizzled hair. 'Dragon-burn,' she said. 'Lo, get the first aid box.'

Lo lifted the box down from the dresser and handed it to Mrs Lind. As he did so, he said something to her in a low voice. I caught the words 'strangers' and 'Big Nigel' and

'Grissel' and 'doughnuts'.

Mrs Lind gave Prudence one of her sharp, twinkly looks. 'If you offer a dragon a gift, and they accept it, they will never harm you – unless you try to take the gift back again. Did you know that?'

Prudence shook her head.

'And hardly anyone,' went on Mrs Lind, 'sees the unicorn. Most people only see what they expect to see. They look at Big Nigel, and they see a horse. You must be … unusual.'

Great, I thought. *Prudence gets to be Unusual, while I'm ordinary, boring Most People.* I didn't want to be *Most People.* I wanted to be different.

Rummaging in the first aid box with her one good hand, Mrs Lind held up a small glass jar.

'Cucumber and alicorn. My grandmother's recipe. You just rub it in and it stops the stinging.' She looked thoughtfully at Prudence. 'We could do with some extra help while my arm heals. There's a lot to do. Some of it's messy, some of them bite, and I can't pay you very much. I don't suppose you want a job?'

'Yes!' breathed Prudence. Her face had gone as pink as her dragon-burnt cheek – as if somebody had given her the best present ever. 'Oh, please, yes!'

No! I thought. *Oh, please, no!* Part of me wished that Grissel had cooked her to a crisp. I wanted Wormestall to go on being my secret. I didn't want it muddled up with the rest of my life. I especially didn't want it muddled up with Prudence.

'She might bring those men back,' I said, meanly. 'She might tell them stuff.'

'I won't,' said Prudence. 'I wouldn't. I swear it. Not ever.'

'They might come back anyway,' I said. 'For another look. Do you think they believed Mrs Wednesday was a cow?'

'She is a cow – sort of.' Lo helped himself to an orange off the hat, and started peeling it. 'It's an extinct sort, that's all. They won't think of that. And they won't have noticed Big Nigel. They're not the type of people to know a unicorn when they see one. There's no reason for them to come back. Why does that fellow have a hook?'

The light died out of Prudence's eyes. 'Mr Mintzer used to work in a zoo. He was Head Reptile Keeper. Until a crocodile bit off his hand.'

'Serves him right,' I said. 'Three cheers for the crocodile. What happened to the hand?'

'He had it stuffed. Diamond – my stepmother – made it into a tie rack for him.'

I tried to imagine a row of spotty bow ties, hanging neatly on a stuffed hand. 'That crocodile – was its name Long Sally?'

Prudence shook her head. 'Sally was a snake, a Burmese python. She was famous, the biggest snake in the country. Then she disappeared. They never found out what happened to her, but I know it was Mr Mintzer who took her. He stole her for Diamond. But Sally wasn't enough.' She squeezed her hands together, biting her lip. 'There's a competition, you see. For taxidermists. The winner gets the Golden Brain Spoon.'

'What's a brain spoon?' I wanted to know.

'It's for spooning out brains, of course,' said Prudence. 'Taxidermists use them. Diamond's desperate to win the Golden Brain Spoon. She's looking for something new to stuff. Something that hasn't been stuffed before. Like the Squermington Wyrm.'

CHAPTER NINE

Diamond Pye wasn't the only person looking for Mortifer.

People were getting twitchy.

Mrs Chen from the Golden Pearl takeaway said she had seen a Chinese dragon scavenging in the bins behind the restaurant. A little boy called Ryan and his sister both said that they had definitely seen a Very Big Snakey Thing curled up asleep on their trampoline. Something left long, winding tracks in the grass up at the golf course, as well as a large poop next to the ninth hole. There was a Poop Expert talking about it on the news. He reckoned it was definitely snake, although it was much bigger than normal, and he was a bit surprised that it had beansprouts and noodles in it.

'With the number of missing pets still rising,' said the TV reporter, looking very serious, 'the question is, does the Squermington Wyrm eat people?'

A lot of kids weren't allowed out after that. The streets were quieter than usual and the park was almost empty, except for Daisy standing on her bench, waving her walking stick and shouting about plagues of frogs and the human race being eaten by the Caterpillar. Police helicopters circled overhead. Everyone agreed: it was time somebody did something, before the worst happened.

Mum didn't ground me, but she wasn't happy about me going to Wormestall.

'I don't like the thought of you being out by yourself,' she said. 'Not with that Thing about.'

'I'm not by myself. There's Mrs Lind and Lo,' I told her. 'And now,' I added gloomily, 'there's Prudence.'

Mum was standing on her head in the bathroom, with her toes pointing at the ceiling. The bath was full of all our dirty clothes. The washing machine was still broken.

'Who's Prudence?'

'She's in my class. She's new. She lives in that big white house on High Holly Hill.' I had ridden past it on my bike, and knew it was hers for two reasons. Firstly, there was a shiny pink sports car parked in the drive. Secondly, there was a sign outside the gate saying:

**DON'T SAY GOODBYE TO YOUR DEAD
WHY NOT HAVE THEM STUFFED INSTEAD?**
Pye's Pet-stuffing Service
Taxidermist of the Year Runner-up
No Job Too Large

'The Pyes' house? Have they come back?' Mum was surprised. 'That house has been empty for years. I knew Daniel Pye way back, before you were born. We went to yoga class together. A nice man – never said very much, but he had kind eyes. He had a job in a museum somewhere, and a wife with amazing red hair. I remember they were expecting a baby – your friend Prudence, I suppose. The next thing I heard, his wife was dead, poor Daniel, and he had moved away to London. I don't know what happened to him after that.'

'I do,' I said. 'He married an evil taxidermist, and then he was killed by a hippopotamus. Prudence lives with her stepmother. And she's not my friend.'

Just then, Steve and Debbie from Next Door came round to ask if we'd seen their cat, but we hadn't. Which was odd because he's nearly always asleep on our ironing board.

I told Mrs Lind about the police helicopters and the TV reporter. She said that basilisks were like dragons and unicorns. They had had a lot of practice at hiding, over the centuries, and they were very good at it.

'Mortifer will be all right,' she said. But you could see she wasn't sure. She had that look in her eyes that Mum has when the Electricity Bill comes.

'Don't be worried,' I told her. 'We just have to find him before anybody else does.'

Mrs Lind put her hands on my shoulders. 'It was a lucky

day when you came to Wormestall, George,' she said. 'I belong here at the Farm and it's difficult for me to leave. Lo goes looking for Mortifer when he can, but he has to take Grissel out for her exercise at night and he's not happy being around people by day. We need somebody who can go between here and Out There.' She waved her hand at the world beyond Wormestall. 'Somebody who belongs in both places. The Right Person. As soon as I saw you, I knew that was you.'

Prudence might be Unusual, but I was the Right Person. That was good enough for me.

Prudence and I didn't see much of each other at Wormestall. We were too busy. My auroch-milking skills improved, until I was almost as quick as Lo. I threw raw meat to Donald and Jemima and carried buckets of pony nuts to the eohippus – pygmy prehistoric ponies the size of cocker spaniels, with toes instead of hooves, and gravy-coloured stripes on their legs. I learned where the flock of archaeopteryx laid their eggs in the orchard, when they weren't crashing clumsily from branch to branch between the apple trees.

'It's not as if they'd ever hatch,' said Lo, biting into a fried-egg sandwich. 'They're not fertile. We think a fox ate the male.'

I remembered the odd, long-legged creature with the beak full of teeth which I had seen on my very first visit to Wormestall. Part-bird, part-dinosaur.

'Actually,' I said, 'I think you'll find him living in Wyvern

Chase Woods.'

I was mostly in charge of the 'extinct' animals, while Prudence saw to the others, the ones that were supposed to belong in myths and legends. She mucked out Grissel and Crackling Rose, took care of Big Nigel, who even let her comb his mane and tail, and threw fish to the kraken. We took turns giving the Ping Feng piglet its bottle, and spooning porridge and honey into Tail-biter. It's not easy feeding something that won't take its tail out of its mouth. You get very sticky.

Sometimes, watching Prudence go in and out of the dragon's stable, I felt a little bit jealous, but I couldn't help noticing she often came out of the stable rather dragon-burnt around the edges. And anyway – I had the ichthyosaur.

I had forgiven it for trying to eat me. You can't blame an animal for being hungry. I didn't dare get in the water with it, but I was teaching it tricks. Heaving a smelly bucket of fish up the tree with me, I would sit on the stump of broken branch, dangling a mackerel at arm's length, and whistle. The surface of the water would tremble as the ichthyosaur woke from its doze beneath the duckweed. Then, quite suddenly, it would shoot like a speeding arrow, leaving a long V behind it in the water, and leap to snatch the fish between its chainsaw jaws before diving back into the water with a mighty splash. It was awesome – just as good as a killer whale – although I never watched it without a little shiver, remembering how close I'd come to being an ichthyosaur-snack.

Our training sessions were a secret. I didn't tell anyone, especially not Prudence. I still wasn't properly talking to Prudence – not if I could help it.

Sometimes, I couldn't help it.

Like the time in the middle of a Science lesson, when a tooth fell out of Prudence's pocket.

We were supposed to be labelling a diagram of the parts of a flower. Prudence had a cold. She gave one of those exploding sneezes and pulled out a tissue. Something dropped onto the floor by her feet, so I glanced down to see what it was.

'George Drake! What on earth's the matter?'

Miss Thripps had been writing on the whiteboard. Now she turned round to stare at me. I changed my yelp of surprise into a cough. Everyone was staring at me, so I covered the thing on the floor with my foot. Prudence bent down to pick it up, then put it calmly back in her pocket. At Break, I went looking for her.

She wasn't hard to find. She was where she always was, leaning against the climbing frame, reading a book.

'*What* was that?' I demanded.

Prudence took her hand out of her pocket. I looked at the object lying on her palm. It was about a finger's length, curved, clear as crystal – and very sharp. A tooth.

'I found it in the woods,' she told me. 'On my way home

from Wormestall that first day, when you took the bike. Mrs Lind says Grissel's losing her teeth all over the place because .of being old, and because of all the sweet stuff she eats. She said I could keep it.'

Slightly envious. I wondered if I could persuade the ichthyosaur to spit out a tooth.

'Be careful,' was all I said. 'You'd better hide it. Supposing Mintzer or your stepmother sees?'

The trouble was, after that, Prudence seemed to think we'd stopped Not Talking. She kept popping up beside me when I was being goalie in the playground, or behind me in the lunch queue.

'Don't you think that cloud looks like a flying dragon?' she'd say, or 'Don't forget to save your apple core for Big Nigel', or 'It's your turn to feed Tail-biter today. I've still got porridge in my hair from yesterday.'

People began to notice. Josh and Matt started making jokes. The girls were worse. Somebody put a piece of paper in my pencil case with a heart drawn on it and a G and a P. Mum found another one when she emptied my PE bag. Harry and Frank thought it was funny, and they started on at me as well. Chants of 'George likes Prudence. Prudence likes Geor-orge!' followed me wherever I went.

I hadn't liked her to start with. Now I liked her even less.

And then, suddenly, Prudence wasn't there.

For three days in a row, she didn't come to school. She

hadn't been seen at Wormestall, either.

'Something's wrong, I know it,' declared Mrs Lind. She had boiled up a new batch of De-petrifaction Ointment and lugged it out to the stables, where she was experimenting on the stone rabbit. She had covered it from nose to tail in green slime, while we coughed and gasped in the fumes, but it still wasn't showing any signs of de-petrifying.

'She's probably just sick,' I suggested. 'Aisha puked in the bus on the way back from swimming the other day. Prudence was sitting next to her.'

Mrs Lind shook her head. 'It's something else. Something worse. You know, this rabbit really ought to be showing signs of life by now.' She poked it, and frowned. 'Not even the twitch of a whisker. I'll run out of rue at this rate. Lo, are you positive that it was weasel wee you gave me? Not stoat ... or ferret?'

'Mmm,' said Lo. He was writing a label to go around the latest stone animal's neck, and not really listening. 'Number 35 Ashmole Road. Or was it 33?'

'Hey, I live at 33 Ashmole Road!' I looked at the stone cat at his feet. 'And that's Next Door's Cat!'

'Maybe you could call by Prudence's house on your way home, George,' suggested Mrs Lind. 'Just to check nothing's wrong?'

I wasn't keen on the idea.

'What if Mr Mintzer's there? He wants to feed me to the Squermington Wyrm.'

'He'll have to find it first,' said Mrs Lind.

Mortifer was still at large. He had last been seen by a frightened waiter at the Star of India, scavenging leftover chicken biryani out of the bins in the middle of the night. The waiter had rung 999, but by the time Emergency Services arrived, the basilisk had gone. So had the biryani.

I tried to think of an excuse, but there wasn't one. Which is how I found myself standing on Prudence's gravel drive, staring at her door knocker. The door knocker stared back at me: a real stuffed fox's head, with a brass ring clamped between its teeth. I didn't really want to touch it, but I'd promised. I raised my hand and knocked.

Nobody came, except for a skinny cat, which jumped off the wall and sat down to clean its tail in a patch of sunlight. I was just turning to go when I heard the scrape of a key in the lock.

'Nnnghhh?'

It was Mr Mump, filling up the whole doorway. The cat came to rub against his legs. 'Unghh,' he said. 'Betty.'

He bent down to scratch her ears, but she sniffed at his hands and walked away with her tail in the air.

'This is for Prudence.' Miss Thripps had given us a Maths worksheet for homework. Generously, I was giving mine to Prudence. I'd had to think of something, to give me a reason for being there. 'Is she all right?'

'Proooodence,' repeated Mr Mump, squinting at the worksheet, which was full of questions about hexagons and cuboids and triangular prisms.

'Yes,' I said. 'Is she sick?'

'Proooodence.'

We weren't getting very far.

'Never mind,' I told him. 'I'll come back another time. Or I'll see her at school. Tell you what, I'll write a note.' Taking a pencil out of my schoolbag, I tore a sheet out of my homework diary and wrote: *Are you dead or something? Mrs Lind wants to know.* I handed it to Mr Mump. 'Can you give her that? And the worksheet has to be handed in on Monday. Thanks.'

I was turning to go when Mump grabbed my arm.

'Nnnghh,' he grunted. 'Come.'

He yanked me into the house, and the door slammed shut behind me.

'I didn't know you had a dog,' I said, putting out my hand to greet a fat black Labrador with a greying muzzle.

When the dog didn't move, I realized someone had turned him into a coffee table. I snatched my hand back. The sheepskin rugs on the floor still had their heads attached and at the foot of the stairs an enormous polar bear balanced on its back legs, wearing a top hat. There was a grand piano in one corner; on top of it stood a penguin, with a lampshade where its face should have been, and a pair of candlesticks made out of two white rats. Above the piano, a gigantic silver fish swung from the ceiling.

It was even bigger than Mump.

I stared at it. 'Is that a *shark*?'

'Nnnghh.' Mump tugged on my arm. 'Piano tuna.'

He marched me all the way through the house and out of the French windows on the other side, across a lawn and through a gate in a brick wall. The air smelled of swimming pool.

Diamond Pye was floating in one of those inflatable rubber armchairs. Mr Mintzer sat in a deckchair, polishing his hook. Beside him was one of those old-fashioned prams, with big silver wheels and a hood. I looked at it in surprise. Prudence hadn't said anything about a baby.

'I know you!' The long, wet hair streaming over Diamond's shoulders was blueberry blue this time. So was the lollipop she took out of her mouth when she saw me. 'You're the boy who saw the Squermington Wyrm!'

She paddled her chair to the edge of the pool. 'Die,' she said.

I blinked at her. Was that an order?

'Di. Short for Diamond. Diamond Pye.' She stretched out her right hand. I didn't want to shake it, but I didn't have much choice. It was quite difficult getting close enough without falling in the water. Her nails were long, painted turquoise and glittery.

'I brought Prudence's homework,' I said. 'Is she ill?'

Diamond licked her lollipop. She had a very pointy tongue. Right now, it was bright blue.

'Are you Prue's friend? I didn't know she had any. She's a very unfriendly girl.'

Only to you, I thought. Then I wondered why I was

sticking up for Prudence, even if it wasn't out loud.

'She must have been telling him things,' said Mintzer. 'He knows too much.'

Diamond gave her tinkly wind-chime laugh. 'I'm sure he's too sensible to believe silly stories. Do you have sisters?' she asked me. I nodded. 'Then you know what girls can be like.' She sighed. 'I'm afraid that Prudence is not a truthful person. Tell me – what do you think of people who tell lies?'

I could feel my face getting hot, which was silly because I hadn't told any lies. Letting her think Prudence and I were friends wasn't *exactly* lying. She was looking at me, waiting.

'Well?'

'Lying's bad,' I muttered.

'Very bad,' agreed Diamond. 'If you lie you get found out, and then you have to take the consequences. Which is why, I'm afraid, you can't see Prudence today. She is being punished.'

'Punished!'

'She only has herself to blame,' said Diamond. 'Her parents are dead, you know. I am all she has. It is my duty to teach her a lesson. Until she admits that she was lying, she must stay where she is.'

Wherever that was. I glanced back at the house, wondering what Prue had said.

Diamond read my mind.

'Silly stories. About fabulous animals. Dragons – that sort of thing.'

'*What?*' I couldn't help it. It burst out of me.

'All nonsense, of course.' Diamond had taken her sunglasses off and was watching me. 'Are you a truthful boy?'

'Mmm.' Why did I get the feeling that I was about to fall into a trap?

'You said you saw the Wyrm. Have you seen anything else? Like ... a dragon?'

I shook my head so hard, it made me dizzy. '*No!*' Sometimes – extra-specially important times – you have to lie. 'Dragons don't exist – everyone knows that!'

'There are other things.' Diamond leant back in her armchair, her eyes on my face. 'Things that might – or might not – be extinct. You haven't seen any of those, either?'

'He was hanging about at that farm.' Mintzer scowled at me. 'There was something not right about that place – something not right about that cow!'

'That's poppycock!' I borrowed Mum's word. 'Mrs Wednesday's a rare breed of cow, that's all. It's just a farm.'

'I'm very interested in rare breeds.' Diamond stretched out her legs, admiring her blue toenails. 'I would like to come and look around, when I get the time. I am very busy with my *magnum opus* – my greatest work. It is not yet complete. There is one thing missing. When I find it, I shall win the Golden Brain Spoon and be Taxidermist of the Year – you'll see!'

You could tell she was excited: she was gripping the arm of her rubber chair so hard her fingernails had dug a hole in it. I could see the little stream of bubbles rising as the air came out.

'Are you interested in taxidermy, boy? Don't you think it's a wonderful thing to be able to cheat Time and Death, and preserve the living form for ever, as a Work of Art?'

'Mmm,' I said again. She hadn't noticed, but the blow-up chair was definitely beginning to wilt.

'A taxidermist can create things that Mother Nature never dreamed of. Look at my baby.' The lollipop was pointing at the pram. 'Go on – look. She doesn't bite!'

I didn't like being within range of Mintzer's hook, but I did what I was told and peered under the hood of the pram.

'Oh!' I said. My step backwards nearly sent me into the pool.

'Show him, Mintzer!' ordered Diamond.

I didn't want to see any more. The wrinkled, leathery little monkey face under the pram's hood, with its empty eye sockets and stretched skin and yellow teeth, had been shocking enough. When Mintzer pulled back the blanket, I couldn't help gaping. Diamond's mummified baby had a tail like a fish.

'Isn't she beautiful?' cooed Diamond.

No. She's the ugliest thing I've ever seen in my whole life.

I just managed not to say it.

'She's a Feejee mermaid,' said Diamond. 'Half monkey, half fish. She is very old. I found her in an antique shop. I never had a baby of my own. I don't count Prudence. She is too big and too sulky. So I have my little mermaid. Have you never wanted to be a mermaid, boy?'

'No,' I said, honestly. 'Never.'

'I have,' said Diamond, dreamily splashing her feet in the water. 'A mermaid with a beautiful silvery tail.' The chair was shrinking quite fast now. 'I shall make one, some day. But I shan't use a monkey. I can't help thinking it would work better with a real person. A girl ... or a boy. A mer-boy.'

She sucked her lollipop, looking thoughtfully at me, as if she might be measuring me. I could feel the goosebumps rising on my arms.

'I ... um ... I think I'd better go home now,' I said.

'Oh, there's no need to hurry,' said Diamond, taking her lollipop out of her mouth. 'Wait—'

But at that moment, with a last *pffff* of escaping air, the inflatable chair deflated and Diamond disappeared under water. The last thing I saw, as I took to my heels and ran, was a froth of bubbles and her blue hair streaming out around her like seaweed.

Nobody came after me. Mintzer and Mump had both rushed to the side of the pool to rescue the sinking, spluttering Diamond. I raced across the lawn and through the house.

'Sorry.' I apologized to a sheep's head as I tripped over it. 'And I'm sorry she turned you into a rug. I'm sorry for you *all*.'

Whatever it took, I wasn't going to let Diamond Pye get her hands on the animals of Wormestall. She'd have Dido turned into a lamp and Mingus into a candlestick in no time. I didn't want to think about what she might do to the others.

The cat was cleaning her whiskers on the bonnet of the pink car. She didn't seem to have noticed the furry paw hanging from the driver's mirror.

'I'd be careful, if I were you,' I warned her. 'This isn't a nice house!'

As I was leaving, something made me look up:

PLEH

There it was, written in what looked like toothpaste on an upstairs window. I knew what it said. Prudence wasn't very good at mirror writing. She had remembered to turn the letters round, but not the whole word. PLEH – HELP.

Behind all the toothpaste, I could see the pale blur of a face. She pressed her hands against the glass, mouthing something at me. I turned away. If Prudence had been blabbing about Wormestall, betraying its secrets, then she deserved everything she got. I didn't care if Diamond turned her into a mermaid. She wasn't getting any PLEH from me.

CHAPTER TEN

The next morning, as Miss Thripps shut the register with her usual snap, Prudence limped into class. She wasn't wearing uniform and her hair was all over the place. There was blood trickling down from her knee into her sock.

'Prudence Pye, you're late. And you look like you've just crawled through a hedge backwards. Where's your school uniform? And where's your sick note?'

Prudence pretended to look in her pockets. I knew she didn't have a sick note.

Miss Thripps rolled her eyes to the ceiling, and told her to go and sit down.

I could feel Prudence's eyes on me. She was trying to get me to look at her. I kept my head bent over my drawing of the Squermington Wyrm.

Halfway through Literacy, she passed me a note:

Diamond knows.

Miss Thripps had her back turned, writing on the whiteboard. I passed the note back:

I know she knows. You told her.

'I did *not*!'

She said it out loud. Miss Thripps spun round.

'Who was that?'

Everybody looked at Prudence.

'Prudence Pye, was that you?'

'I *didn't!*' Prudence was looking at me, not at Miss Thripps.

Miss Thripps' lips tightened. 'I'm writing your name on the board. Twice. Once for shouting out, once for lying.'

At Break, Miss Thripps made Prue stay behind and sharpen all the pencils – which at least meant she couldn't follow me around the playground, wanting to talk.

When the bell rang for the end of Break, I had to go to the toilet. I'd be late back in class, but I was desperate. I was in there, trying to be quick, when somebody on the other side of the door said, 'George, I know that's you.'

'What are you *doing*? These are the *Boys'* Toilets,' I hissed. 'Get out! You're not *allowed*!'

'You've got to listen,' said Prudence. 'This was the only way I could think of. Don't try and get past me. You can't. I'm leaning against the door and I'm heavier than you. George, I didn't tell about Wormestall. I swear I didn't. They found the tooth. They asked me all sorts of questions. Then they searched my bedroom, and they found ... other stuff.'

'What?'

'This,' said Prudence, unhappily.

She passed a ball of paper under the door. I smoothed out the crumpled sheets and my heart sank.

She was much better at drawing than I am. When I draw things, you can't always tell what they're meant to be. Prudence's sketches were very lifelike. *Too* lifelike. Grissel, Big Nigel, the kraken in the toilet, Mingus on Mrs Lind's hat, Dido on her eggs: they were all there, as clear as day.

'But they can't have thought they were real? Diamond said you'd been making stuff up. She said you'd been telling lies.'

'I *did* lie. I had to. I told them I'd made it all up – that the animals were my imaginary friends. They didn't believe me, so they locked me in the Trophy Room until I told the truth.'

'They locked you *where*?'

'In the— Oh, it doesn't matter. But, George, you do believe me, don't you? I didn't tell. Why would I tell Diamond *anything*? I wish that hippopotamus had fallen on her, not on Dad.'

'It *fell* on him? What was a hippopotamus doing up in the air?'

'It was being moved by a crane. It was for a display in the museum where he worked. That's how he met Diamond. Next to the stuffed elephant. She told him how she'd always wanted to stuff something really big. He told her he had a giraffe that was falling to pieces – she said she'd fix it for him. Next thing, they were getting married.

'George, you have to get to Wormestall and warn Mrs Lind. I can't go, in case I'm followed. They still don't know for sure there's anything there, but they're suspicious. I heard Mintzer telling Diamond that Mrs Wednesday's head would look good hanging on the wall in the Trophy Room. She said she'd go and have a look, and if she sees ...' I heard her swallow a sob. 'Oh, George, you don't know what she's like! She really wants to win the Golden Brain Spoon this year. And when she wants something, she'll do anything – *anything* – to get it.'

'All right,' I said. 'I believe you. Now will you let me out? You know something?' I added, as the door swung open. 'Miss Thripps was right. You do look as if you've been dragged through a hedge backwards.'

'More downwards,' said Prudence, 'than backwards. I escaped. I had to get to school, to warn you, so I climbed out of the window.'

I looked at her with respect. 'An *upstairs* window?'

'There's a ledge. And a creepery plant thing growing up the wall, but it wasn't as strong as I hoped. I fell the last bit. Flower beds aren't as soft as you'd think.'

'You're brave.' I meant it.

Prudence shook her head. 'No, I'm not. Diamond scares me. Diamond's a *lot* more dangerous than climbing out of windows.'

Miss Thripps wrote both our names up on the board for being late into class.

At lunch, I told Josh and Matt that I couldn't play football: I had something to do. Prudence and I had an Emergency What-To-Do-Next Meeting. It wasn't a very useful meeting. By the time the bell rang, we still didn't know what to do next.

At the end of the day, our names were still on the board. Somebody had drawn a heart in between them, but I had more important stuff than that to worry about.

'Where will you go?' I asked Prudence, as we zipped up our schoolbags. 'You can't go home. They'll shut you up again. You can come to my house, if you like.'

She shook her head. 'You must go to Wormestall and tell them what's happened. Say it's all my fault, and I'm really, really sorry and—' She gave a sudden gasp. Clutching her bag to her chest, she pointed to the window.

Our classroom is upstairs. It looks out over the school gates. Parked on the road outside was a pink sports car. Leaning against it was Diamond Pye. He hair was lime-green, rolled up in a complicated knot and skewered into place with what looked like chopsticks. As the flood of children poured out through the gates, she sucked on a green lollipop, watching and waiting.

'Quick!' I decided. 'We'll go out the other way. Through the Infants' door.'

Junior School kids aren't really allowed in the Infants' playground. Luckily for us, a little girl had just fallen off the monkey bars. She was screaming her head off and bleeding everywhere, so it was easy to creep past unnoticed and out into the narrow side road, where we couldn't be seen from the main school gates.

'Come on.' I grabbed Prudence's arm. 'We'll go to my mum's shop. You'll be safe there. We can hide you in the back.'

Prudence hung back. 'Your mum doesn't even know me. Won't she mind?'

'Why should she? Anyway, she knew your dad. They used to stand on their heads together. Come on – it's not far, if we cut through the park.'

It was raining, for the first time in days. What with the weather and people being afraid of the Wyrm, there was nobody around. Nobody except Crazy Daisy, who was standing on her bench, as usual, one arm up in the air like a traffic policeman, with Doom yapping at her feet.

'Any minute now, she'll start shouting at us,' I warned Prudence.

But she didn't. We walked right up to her and she still didn't. It was pretty obvious why.

'Stone.' Prudence reached out to touch her. 'She's made of stone.'

Mortifer.

Prudence and I looked at each other, then at the bushes.

'How long do you think she's been like this?' asked Prudence.

'I don't know,' I said. 'It can't be long, or someone would have seen and there'd be a fuss.'

Mortifer could not be far away. My heart was beating

rather hard. Better not to look too hard at the bushes, in case something looked back at me. What does it feel like, being turned into stone? I wasn't in a hurry to find out.

Prudence was on her knees, burrowing in her school bag.

'What are you doing?'

'We had better put these on, just in case.' She handed me a pair of sunglasses with mirrored lenses. 'They're Diamond's. She's got so many, she'll never notice.'

The glasses were much too big. Prudence looked like a cross between a film star and a mutant frog. It felt stupid wearing sunglasses in the rain, but safer.

'We need to move her,' I said, nodding at Daisy. 'Before anyone comes.'

'Poor Doom,' said Prudence, watching the little dog jump on and off the bench, whimpering and whining. 'Why didn't *he* get turned to stone?'

'He was probably off after a squirrel; he's always chasing things. How are we going to do this?' I gave Daisy a push, but she didn't even wobble. 'I can't shift her. She's too heavy.'

'Look.' Prudence pointed at the fountain. 'Over there.'

In the middle of the fountain was a statue of a fat little boy riding a large fish. The water was supposed to come out of the fish's mouth, but that hadn't happened for years. Both boy and fish were covered in pigeon droppings, and the water in the pool was green and murky. Sometimes, people threw in a coin. More often they threw in rubbish. Today, someone had thrown in a supermarket trolley. They probably weren't meaning to be helpful when they did it, but it was just what we needed.

Prudence wheeled the trolley up to the bench and held it steady. I climbed up behind Daisy and pushed as hard as I could.

Daisy teetered, but stayed where she was.

'Try again,' instructed Prudence. 'Harder.'

I shoved and shoved, and finally … *chwannng*! Daisy toppled head first into the trolley.

'Goal!' I punched the air.

'I feel a bit bad about her being upside down,' said Prudence.

'It's good for her,' I said. 'It's yoga.'

'Where are we going to put her?' asked Prudence. 'We need to be quick. Listen – there are people coming!'

'We'll tip her in the bushes.'

'We can't just dump her! And she'll stick out. Someone's bound to notice.'

'All right, then – we'll take her to Wormestall. We can push her there in the trolley.'

'People will see,' objected Prudence.

'We'll cover her up. There'll be something in Mum's shop we can use. Come on!'

There's a mermaid in the window of The Mermaid's Cave. Not a real one, obviously. It's a shop dummy, wearing a long wig and a cloth tail that Harry once wore to a fancy-dress party. She sits on this fake polystyrene rock, sad and dusty, with shells and plastic weed and bits of fishing net all around

her, and puts off the customers. But Mum likes her.

As soon as you open the shop door, all these wind-chimes start tinkling, and then you're swallowed up in this cloud of smelly incense and weird whale song. Mum wasn't there. Harry was behind the counter, reading the paper and wearing headphones so she didn't have to listen to the whales.

'Hello,' she said, taking out one headphone. 'Mum's gone to her yoga class. Don't I know that dog?'

Prudence was carrying Doom in her arms. We had parked Daisy at the back of the shop, where nobody goes.

'We're just taking him for a walk,' I said, vaguely.

I was looking at Mum's crystal ball. She bought it at a car boot sale from a woman who said it had belonged to her great-great-grandmother who was a fortune-teller, and that it really worked. Nobody believed her except Mum, who paid her a lot of money and keeps the ball in the shop, on a little table covered in red velvet.

'Harry, can we borrow that cloth? We'll bring it back.'

Harry looked a bit surprised, but she didn't say we couldn't.

I had gathered up the velvet and was putting the ball back in place when I glanced out of the window – just in time to see a convertible pink sports car, pulling up on the double yellow lines outside. I froze. *Diamond's guessed*, I thought. *She knows Prudence is with me. And she's found out this is Mum's shop*. I grabbed Prudence and made a dash for the bead curtain at the back of the shop. Behind it there's a poky little room with a cracked washbasin, where Mum keeps her spare stock.

'Harry, if somebody comes in and asks – someone with a lollipop – you haven't seen us!' I said, urgently. 'We're not here! It really, really matters. It's Life or Death!'

'Oh? What's it worth?' said Harry.

Shoving Prudence and Doom through the bead curtain, I pulled a packet of Cheesy Snake Snacks out of my pocket. They had been there since Break, when Fazal had swapped them for my Manchester United pencil sharpener. They were a bit squashed, but Harry loves Cheesy Snake Snacks. She shrugged and held out her hand.

We were only just in time. The beads were still rattling when the wind chimes tinkled.

'What a quaint little shop,' said a voice I did not at all want to hear.

'Nnnghh,' said Mump. 'Smell!'

'That's the incense,' explained Harry. 'It's called Sea Mist. Can I help you?'

'I've lost my little daughter.' Diamond heaved a big pretend sigh, as if she really cared. 'I've been looking everywhere for her. Eleven years old. Red hair. Not that pretty, I'm afraid – rather like a startled antelope. Have you seen her?'

Crouched behind a stack of cardboard boxes, Prudence and I held our breath.

Harry didn't let us down.

'There was a man who looked a lot like a walrus,' she said.

'And a woman who looked a bit like a mouse. No one who looked like any kind of deer. Sorry.'

'Oh dear,' said Diamond. 'My little girl is very precious to me, you see. Children are *such* a worry!'

'You need to relax,' said Harry. 'You should buy some incense sticks – lavender's good for stress – and a nice whale song CD. Eleven is quite old. I expect your daughter can look after herself. My brother's eleven and we don't fuss about *him*.'

'Ah, yes.' Diamond's voice was as smooth as custard. 'Your little brother ...'

She was interrupted by Doom. He had been growing more and more fidgety in Prudence's arms; now he broke free and disappeared through the bead curtain. We could hear his claws as he scampered across the shop floor.

'Nnnghh,' said Mump. 'Dog!'

'Just the right size for a footstool,' said Diamond. 'Or a hot-water bottle cover.'

'No!' That was Harry's voice. 'Not in the window! Bad dog! Oh, gross! That stinks!'

Even the Sea Mist couldn't hide it. The smell drifted all the way to the back of the shop. Our noses wrinkled. Doom must have been desperate.

'If you wanted to have it stuffed,' said Diamond, 'I could do it quite cheaply. Most of my customers agree their pets are much less trouble that way.'

There was a flurry of yapping, followed by muffled growls. We heard Harry cry out, and her footsteps as she ran out from behind the counter.

'It's attacking the mermaid!' she cried. 'Stop it! Drop it! Bad, bad dog! Oh, look what you've done to her tail!'

Wind-chimes were tinkling. It wasn't the door this time; it was Diamond laughing. 'I wouldn't worry about that tatty old mermaid,' she told Harry. 'I can make you a new one, much more lifelike. But first, I need to find my daughter ...'

'They've gone,' said Harry, parting the bead curtain a few minutes later. 'You can come out now – and clear up the mess that dog has made!'

We got rid of the dog-do, and smoothed out the sand, but there was nothing we could do to hide what had happened to the mermaid. Her tail was in shreds. She looked as if she had been attacked by a shoal of piranha. All we could do was sweep up all the little scraps of silver, and hope that Mum came back nice and chilled from her yoga.

Harry gave us both a Cheesy Snake Snack, which was kind of her in the circumstances. Cheesy Snake Snacks don't look much like snakes, but there's a picture of a snake on the packet: a curly-wurly brightly-coloured one.

'Do you think the Squermington Wyrm looks like that?' said Harry, with her mouth full. 'Have you heard? It's got bored with dogs and cats. It's eating children now.'

'It's *what*?'

'See for yourself.' Harry pushed the newspaper across the counter.

There, on the cover, was a picture of a round-faced little girl with bunches.

Squermington Echo

SNATCHED FROM HER OWN GARDEN!

SQUERMINGTON WYRM STEALS CHILD!

Little Lily Lamprey was playing happily in the garden at her home in Blackberry Terrace when she suddenly disappeared.

'It was that dreadful Wyrm that took her,' said her mother, Mrs Lamprey. 'I know it was.'

'Someone needs to hunt that monster down and kill it,' said Mr Spike Hardman, who lives next door to the Lampreys. 'If I find it, I'll chop it into a thousand pieces.'

Police are searching the area for clues.

I pushed the paper back at Harry and picked up my schoolbag.

'Come on,' I told Prudence. 'We have to get to Wormestall. Fast.'

'Wait a minute,' objected Harry. 'You haven't told me what's going on.' She looked at Prudence. 'Was that woman your mother?'

'Stepmother,' corrected Prudence.

'Like the ones in fairy stories, only much, much worse.' I scooped up Doom. 'I'll explain later, Harry. Just eat your Cheesy Snake Snacks.'

CHAPTER ELEVEN

I t's not easy running when you've got a shopping trolley full of petrified woman and a daft dog, and it's pouring with rain. We took turns pushing, swapping over when we got too breathless. The trolley had a wonky wheel – it didn't like going in a straight line and kept wanting to turn left, which made it hard to steer. The wet pavements were slippery. Cars whooshed by, spraying us with puddle water, but at least none of them was pink. The wind got under the red velvet, making it swell and flap. As we turned a corner, a sudden strong gust blew it right off, leaving Daisy's ghostly legs sticking up in the air for everyone to see. Luckily, the only people around were in such a hurry to get where they were going, out of the rain, they didn't look up from under their umbrellas.

By the time we got to Wormestall, we were soaked and exhausted. As we bumped the trolley up the track, the sun was shining. Everywhere else there were grey clouds, but the farm sat under a circle of blue sky. The aurochs were grazing peacefully. Lo was in Big Nigel's field with a bucket of pony nuts and a cheese grater. He rattled the bucket, but the unicorn had seen the grater and cantered away from him, shaking his head and kicking up his back hooves.

'Anyone would think it hurt him, having his horn grated,' said Lo, crossly. 'We need more alicorn. Mrs Lind's bones ache in the wet weather.'

I looked up at the ring of blue sky.

'Is that why you pushed the rain away, to make her feel better?'

Lo shrugged. Nobody ever talked about his tricks with the weather, but it only ever seemed to rain at Wormestall when everybody was busy indoors, or when one of Grissel's fires needed putting out.

'You found her, then,' he said, nodding at Prudence. 'Why is that rabbit barking?'

'It's not a rabbit. It's a dog,' I said. 'His name is Doom and he belongs to Crazy Daisy and she's been turned into stone.' I pulled the cloth off the trolley. 'And here she is. We had to move her before anyone saw. And Mortifer's eaten a little girl, and now people want to chop him into a thousand pieces.'

'I expect he was hungry,' said Lo.

Prudence stroked Doom's ears. 'So ... he does eat people, then? Not just takeaways.'

'Of course he eats people. Why wouldn't he? They're

delicious. You eat meat,' Lo pointed out. 'That dog eats meat. So does Mortifer. There's nothing special about humans. They're made of meat, same as everything else. They just make more fuss about being eaten. You have to feel sorry for basilisks,' he added. 'Think about it. It's not easy when your dinner keeps turning into stone. Their only chance of getting fresh meat is to take it by surprise – maybe when it's sleeping. The easiest thing is to find one that's had too much to drink. They can't see straight, and they fall asleep in odd places. But they don't taste so good. Sweat and vinegar.' Lo made a face. 'Not my favourite flavour.'

Prudence and I looked at each other. Was he joking? You just never knew with Lo.

Mrs Lind was in the kitchen. You could tell, from a long way off, that she had been boiling up another batch of De-petrifaction Ointment. We left Daisy by the back door with Doom to guard her.

The Ping Feng piglet had burrowed under its blanket to escape the stink. The Early Mammal had curled itself around the brim of Mrs Lind's hat, with its head buried under a banana skin. Only Dido seemed unbothered by the fumes, making little *chuck-chuck* noises as she nestled on her eggs, with her eyes half-closed.

'No sense of smell,' said Lo. 'Fortunate bird.'

'I really think it might work this time.' Mrs Lind peered hopefully into the depths of her saucepan. 'Lo owned up. He cheated with the weasel wee. It wasn't a weasel. It was

Mingus. This time, it's the proper stuff.' She smiled at Prudence. 'I am glad George has brought you back to us.'

'Her stepmother locked her up,' I told them. 'Prudence had to climb out of a window. And Diamond thinks we're hiding the Squermington Wyrm. She'll be coming quite soon, and she'll stuff anything she finds. She turns animals into pieces of furniture. She'll probably turn Big Nigel into a sofa.'

'It's all my fault.' Prudence hung her head. 'I should never have come here!'

'Nonsense,' said Mrs Lind, briskly. 'You couldn't help coming. Wormestall is like a magnet – it pulls the people who belong here towards it, and drives off the rest. If your stepmother does come, she can't expect to have it all her own way.'

'But that's exactly what she does expect,' said Prudence, miserably. 'And she's usually right. I should leave.'

'Before you do,' said Lo, handing her the grater, 'you can have a go at Big Nigel. He's keen on you.'

We left Doom at Wormestall, with Daisy. Prudence kissed him goodbye.

'I'd like to take you with me,' she told him. 'But you'd get stuffed in no time.'

We walked back through the woods. I didn't even notice the rustlings and the shadows. I was thinking about Prudence.

'You could go to the police,' I told her. 'I don't think it's allowed – locking children up, when they're meant to be at school. Diamond would get into trouble.'

'Nobody would believe me,' said Prudence. 'She and Mintzer would say I was making it all up. Grown-ups always believe other grown-ups, rather than children. And Diamond's good at pretending to be nice. She's had practice – she fooled my dad.'

'You could run away,' I suggested. 'You could stay at Wormestall. Mrs Lind's not like other grown-ups. She'll believe you.'

Prudence shook her head. 'There'd be a fuss. Mrs Lind wouldn't want that. I used to think about running away,' she admitted. 'When I was little and we lived in London, Dad used to tell me stories about our house here. It was where he lived with Mum, before I was born. After the hippopotamus, when it was just me and Diamond, I used to dream about escaping and coming to live here. It's my house – at least, it will be when I'm eighteen. Then I can tell Diamond to get out and never come back. That's what I think about, when she locks me up. It makes it better.'

'Isn't that rather a long time to wait?' I said 'Eighteen's ages away.'

'Eighty-four months. Two thousand five hundred and fifty-six days, counting one leap year. Sixty-one thousand, three hundred and forty-four hours. Three million, six hundred and eighty thousand, six hundred and forty minutes. Two hundred and twenty million and something seconds. That was on my last birthday – I work it out every year – so it's loads less than that now. There's nothing really dreadful that Diamond can do between now and then. She can't eat me!'

'Sweat and vinegar,' I said. 'I reckon you'd taste better than that.'

It's probably the nicest thing I've ever said to a girl.

Prudence gave me a sideways look. 'Lo doesn't really know what people taste like? I mean ... he's not a *cannibal*. Is he?'

'You're only a cannibal,' I said, 'if you eat your own sort. I'm not totally sure Lo is ... our sort.'

Prudence stared at me. 'You don't think he's *human*?'

'How should I know? It's just that we don't know where he came from – he never says anything about his family, or ever going to school. You have to admit he's ... different.' I thought of the upstairs bedroom, with its bare mattress and drifting feathers. 'The first time I met him, he came in through the window. And have you ever wondered how he gets those stone animals back to Wormestall? I can only just pick up the rabbit rock. And there's that thing he does with the weather ...'

A car shot past us. It wasn't pink, but I heard Prudence's gasp of fright.

'I tell you what,' I suggested 'Come back to my house. I've got a calculator. We can work out how many days and hours and minutes there are left before you can chuck Diamond out. Then I'll teach you how to play *All Star Zombie Smackdown*.'

Prudence looked pleased. I wanted her to stay happy, just

for a bit, so when we reached the Sweet Shop, I stopped.

'Wait a minute,' I told her.

Mrs Lind had paid me for a week's work. I was rich. I didn't even have to save up for a bike any more. The Help Wanted sign had gone from the window, but there were plenty For Sale and Lost cards, including one saying '**Have You Seen This Child?**' underneath a picture of Little Lily Lamprey. I left Prudence outside reading the advertisements while I popped into the shop to buy us both some sweets.

I was only in there for about a minute.

When I came out, she'd disappeared.

I was just in time to see a pink car screaming round the corner at the end of the road. I looked at the number plate: STUFF U

'Prudence Pye's been kidnapped by her stepmother,' I announced, when I got home.

'Poppycock,' said Mum, banging saucepans around. 'I'm not in the mood for fairy stories. That dog you brought into the shop ate half my mermaid. Now what am I going to put in the window? Sit down and eat your supper. It's Mashed Marrow and Mushroom Surprise.'

I looked at the plate she handed me. It was mostly green, with brown lumps that might have been mushroom. Or possibly slug.

'What's the Surprise?' I asked.

'The surprise,' said Mum, 'is that you are going to sit down and eat it. Without another word.'

Prudence wasn't at school the next day.

'Prudence Pye – absent *again*,' complained Miss Thripps. 'She must be very unhealthy!'

'There's nothing wrong with her.' I said. 'She's being kept locked up by her evil stepmother.'

'Don't be ridiculous, George,' snapped Miss Thripps.

Nobody believed me. Which meant that there was only one thing to do.

I had to go and rescue Prudence myself.

I got home from school to find Frank taping a packet of frozen peas to her leg. She had hurt her knee playing netball.

'I'm in excruciatingly awful *agony*,' she said. 'George, you'll have to take Sir Crispin for his walk.'

'No way,' I said. 'You sacked me, remember? And Mrs Poker-Peagrim hates me. She won't let me anywhere near the fat fur-ball.'

'Mrs Poker-Peagrim's gone away. She's visiting her sister. She can't take Sir Crispin because her sister has this huge ferocious cat, and Sir Crispin wets himself every time he sees it. It's only for the weekend, so I said I'd look after him. Except now I can't because *I'm in horrendously horrible pain.*' She made groaning noises to prove it as she stretched out on the sofa and reached for the remote control. 'So you'll have to do it.'

'What if I don't want to?'

I argued until she said that if I walked Sir Crispin she'd

take me bowling. I argued a bit more until she said we could have pizza afterwards. It seemed like a good moment to give in. Mrs Poker-Peagrim's house was on the way to Prudence's. Sir Crispin and I would rescue her together.

'And you have remembered about Mum's birthday, haven't you?' Frank called after me, as I was leaving. 'You haven't forgotten?'

'Of course I haven't forgotten,' I said. 'Er ... when?'

'Tomorrow, snailbrain. Make sure you get her a present. A proper one. Not football stickers, like last year.'

'That was the year before. I gave her a Mars bar last year. Anyway, she liked the football stickers. Dad stuck them on the fridge.'

'Yeah, well, Dad's not here this year, is he? It's her first birthday without him. We have to cheer her up.'

Sir Crispin and I started off at a good pace. He trotted along beside me, stopping every few minutes to sniff about and cock his leg. I wasn't paying much attention: I was busy wondering just how, exactly, we were going to carry out our daring rescue. As he began to get tired, he slowed to a waddle. By the time we turned into Prudence's road, it felt like I was dragging a dead weight. My arm was aching.

'Come on, Frogface.' I gave him a yank. 'The sooner we get there, the sooner we ...'

I turned to look at him and stopped dead. No wonder my arm was aching.

I wasn't pulling a dog along behind me. I was pulling a

lump of stone.

Somewhere along the way, while he was having one of his sniff 'n' widdles, Sir Crispin had found himself eyeball-to-eyeball with a basilisk.

CHAPTER TWELVE

What was I going to tell Frank? Worse, what was I going to tell Mrs Poker-Peagrim?

'Sorry about your dog. Here's a nice doorstop instead.'

I could only hope that Mrs Lind got the De-petrifaction Ointment to work soon, while Frank was still glued to the sofa and Mrs Poker-Peagrim was still at her sister's.

Meanwhile, here I was, with a rock on a lead, at Prudence's house. I looked at the upstairs windows, in case there was a message for me. You could see toothpastey smears still on the glass, but the curtains were drawn and there was no sign of life.

Mump's cat was there, cleaning the tip of her tail. The good news was that there was no pink car in the drive. With luck, that meant that Diamond was out.

It was Mump, again, who opened the door.

'Nnnngh!' he said.

'I've come to see Prudence,' I told him. 'It's very urgent. To do with school.'

You can usually trick grown-ups into thinking something's important if you say it's for school. Not Mump.

'Nnn-nnnghh!' he said firmly, wedging himself into the doorway so that not even a fly could have squeezed past.

I did a bit of quick thinking. Mump was a lot bigger than me and a lot stronger. That did not mean he was any cleverer.

I shrugged my shoulders and turned away, as if I was leaving. Then I pointed at a flower bed just out of Mump's sight.

'Hey!' I said. 'What's that? Wow! It looks like the Squermington Wyrm!'

It was the oldest trick in the playground, but it worked.

'Hnnnghh?'

Frowning, Mump lumbered out from the doorway, peering in the direction of my finger.

It was all I needed. I charged at the doorway and was halfway up the stairs before Mump even realized I'd got past him.

At the top of the stairs, I stopped.

'Prue!' I yelled. 'Where are you?'

'George! George – don't!' Her scared voice came from behind a door down the corridor. 'Get to Wormestall and warn them Diamond's coming. Go, quick – before they—'

'I'm letting you out first,' I told her. 'Just hang on.'

My hand was on the doorknob. 'It's OK – the key's in the door ...'

'All the better to lock you in with,' breathed a voice in my ear.

'George – RUN!' screamed Prudence.

Sometimes, it's not such a bad idea to do what you're told.

I ran. But not fast enough. I choked as something grabbed me around the neck. Spluttering, I put my hands up to my throat and felt cold, hard steel.

'Prue ...' I gasped.

'She's right here,' said Mintzer, pulling me towards him like a hooked fish. 'You can join her if you like. Or even if you don't like.' Turning the key in the lock, he kicked open the door and pushed me through.

There were eyes and teeth and horns all around me. Heads without bodies staring out from every patch of wall. Lions and leopards and panthers and pumas snarled and glared. Different kinds of deer, with antlers like tree branches, stared sadly at nothing through dusty glass eyes. A stuffed eagle hung from the ceiling, talons outstretched, and I nearly tripped over a tiger skin, baring its teeth at my ankles.

'Welcome to the Trophy Room. Magnificent, isn't it?' said Mintzer. He had let go of my neck, but the fingers of his one hand were pinching my arm. 'All shot by Mrs Pye's great-great-grandfather, Sir Waldo Whippenslitt. A great man. There he is, between the kudu and the panther.'

He shoved me towards the photograph hanging on the

wall between a gentle-eyed creature with horns like giant corkscrews, and a black cat that looked as if it was trying to sick up a hairball. It was an old picture: everything in it was tea-coloured. Sir Waldo Whippenslitt had a big gun and a big moustache and was standing with one foot on a dead elephant, looking pleased with himself.

You could see Prudence had been crying: her eyes were red. She was sitting hunched, with her arms around her knees. She couldn't have stood up if she'd wanted to: she was in a cage.

My mouth felt dry. This was worse than I had imagined. Who put children in cages? All I could think of was the witch in Hansel and Gretel, fattening Hansel up for her dinner.

'Here you are, missy,' Mintzer told Prudence. 'Here's your little friend come to play, so you can stop complaining.' Turning to me, he said, 'You can't get her out of there, so don't even try. Mrs Pye's gone to see a woman who wants her racehorse stuffed. She won't be long. You can keep each other company, until she gets home. Then we're off to that run-down old farm you're so keen on. Mrs Pye's very interested to see what you're hiding there. We've some idea already – thanks to Little Miss Arty Pants here. As soon as we find it, we'll catch it, we'll bag it ...' He pointed at a pile of sacks in one corner. 'And then ...' His eyes gleamed as he drew the edge of his hook across his throat.

'No!' I said, furiously. 'Leave Wormestall alone! You're not stuffing anything. I won't let you. I'll ...'

'You'll what?' asked Mr Mintzer. 'I'll leave you to think about it, shall I? *Catch you later, stuffed alligator ...*'

And with a mean, mocking laugh, he was gone, the key scraping in the lock behind him.

I knelt down, tugging at the padlock on the cage door.

'It's no use,' Prudence told me, hopelessly. 'It won't open. Not without the key, and Mump's got that.'

'How long have you been in there?'

'Don't know,' said Prudence. 'Time works differently when you're locked up.'

'They can't keep shut you up like a ... like a hamster! Have they done it before?'

'Loads of times. Whenever I do something bad.'

'They're the ones doing something bad. What do we do now?'

'There's nothing we can do,' said Prue. 'The door's locked and the window's useless – there's nothing to hold on to. If you jumped, you'd break a leg, at least. We'll just have to wait. Sometimes Mump brings me cake. Maybe that'll be our chance.'

So we waited. Time passed.

Prudence looked as if she was dozing, with her head bent and her cheek resting on her knees. I started playing the Million Game. *Something has to happen*, I told myself, *before I get to a million. It always does ...*

By the time something did happen, I had beaten my record. I was up to 4,658 when the door opened and Mr Mump came in, turning the key in the lock behind him.

'Nnngh,' said Mump, setting down a tray. 'Hunngghry.'

He gave us each a glass of milk and a large slice of fruit cake, squashing Prudence's through the bars of the cage. My mouth was too dry to swallow properly. The milk was cold and refreshing, but it made me think of Mrs Tuesday and Mrs Wednesday. I imagined them ending up among all the other horned heads nailed to the wall, and put the glass down again.

'I need to go to the bathroom,' said Prudence. She caught my eye as she said it. I gave her a little nod. Mump was big but he was slow. Once the door was unlocked, we had a chance – just as long as we didn't run into Mintzer.

Mump undid the padlock on the cage and Prudence crawled out. She stood up, and had to grab hold of the kudu's horns to stop herself from falling over.

'My leg's gone to sleep.' She shot me a worried look. A dead leg wasn't going to help our get-away. Mump was unlocking the bedroom door when a horn blared, sharply.

'Nnnghh?' said Mump. Heaving himself over to the window, he pushed it open. I heard the growl of a car engine, and Diamond's raised voice.

'What idiot left a statue in the middle of the drive? How am I supposed to park? Mintzer, get it out of my way!'

Mintzer's footsteps crunched on the gravel. 'I don't know how it got there.' He sounded surprised. 'It wasn't there ten minutes ago. That's odd – it looks just like—'

'Betty!' bellowed Mump, suddenly, making me jump. 'Nnnghh nnnghhh nnnghhh *Betty!*'

He was leaning so far out of the window, he might have fallen if he hadn't been too big to fit.

'Smelly Betty. That's his cat,' whispered Prudence, hopping up and down behind me.

'Not any more she's not.' I peered around Mump's bulk. 'She's a lump of stone now.'

It could only just have happened. Which meant that Mortifer wasn't far away.

Something in the bushes caught my eye: a gleam of gold. A colossal shape was gliding, like squeezed toothpaste, through the shrubbery ...

I wasn't the only one to have seen it.

'It's the Wyrm! Get Great-great-grandfather's gun,' shrieked Diamond. '*Catch it! Bag it! Stuff it!*'

Mump turned round. His face had twisted, and he was making grunting, snuffly noises. Was he *crying*? Hanging on the wall above Sir Waldo's picture was a gun: the same gun as he was holding in the photograph. A gun big enough to kill an elephant. Or a basilisk.

'No!' Prudence clutched Mump's arm. 'No, Mump –

don't! We know someone who can make Smelly Betty better. Wait – please, wait!'

But Mump brushed her off and took down the gun. Outside, I could still see the glint of scales between the bushes. Mump propped the gun on his shoulder and took aim through the open window.

When it really matters, you do things without thinking. I seized the first heavy thing I saw, lifted it and brought it down hard over Mump's head. The gun went off like a crack of thunder. Birds rose out of trees, *cawk-cawking* in alarm, and Mump slumped over the window sill.

'You've killed him!' Prudence's face was white. 'Did he hit Mortifer?'

'I don't think so.' I felt a bit dizzy. I'd never knocked anybody out before. I looked at the bloodstained weapon in my hands, and realized it was Sir Crispin.

'It went that way!' Diamond was shouting at Mintzer. The shot must have missed. '*After it*!'

Mump wasn't moving. Mum wasn't going to be too happy about me being a Murderer; she wanted me to be an Astronaut.

'Poke him,' said Prudence.

'I don't want to poke him. You poke him.'

We both poked him. Mump twitched.

'He must have a very hard head,' I said. 'He's chipped Sir Crispin.'

The door was unlocked. Mump was unconscious. This was our chance.

'Hurry,' said Prudence. 'We'll go out the back ...'

'Oh no, you won't.'

There, in the doorway, stood Mintzer, polishing his hook with his hanky. He closed the door behind him. 'Mrs Pye's not going to be very happy with you two, spoiling Mump's aim like that and scaring off the Wyrm. You'll be back in that cage until Christmas, I shouldn't wonder,' he told Prudence. 'Starting now.'

She backed away from him, but the hook shot out and caught her.

'Leave her alone!' I ordered as he bundled her, wriggling and struggling, back into the cage.

Mintzer kicked out with one of his pointy-toed shoes, catching me on the shin.

'Ouch!' I said.

He laughed and trod on my foot. On purpose.

I was properly angry now. The kudu, with its corkscrew horns, stretched out its neck and looked at me, as if it was trying to tell me something. I had a sudden flashback: Mintzer in the stable yard at Wormestall, pinned between Mrs Wednesday's horns ...

I tore the kudu off the wall and charged.

'Now, wait a minute ...' said Mintzer.

Letting go of Prudence, he took a step backwards, then another, then another, until he was backed up against the door. I didn't stop – and nor did the kudu. Its horns drilled right through the wooden door and out the other side – with Mintzer trapped in between them, his arms pinned to his sides. It was his turn to struggle now, but it wasn't any use.

'Cheers for that,' I told the kudu. I couldn't help thinking it looked a tiny bit more cheerful.

It was a bit awkward having to open the door with Mr Mintzer still attached – the things he said to us weren't very nice – but we got through it and out into the corridor.

'Back stairs,' said Prudence. 'Follow me.'

CHAPTER THIRTEEN

We might have made it if my shoelaces had been done up.

They weren't, because they never are. It's not my fault: my knots just don't stay knotted. People nag me about it all the time – Mum, teachers, everyone. 'Do your shoelaces up, George, or you'll trip.'

I'd never listened, but it turns out they were right. I tripped.

Prudence had just started down the stairs and I was right behind her when I gave a sudden lurch. I had no way of saving myself; my arms were full of Sir Crispin. Together, we went clattering and crashing down the stairs, taking Prudence with us – and making enough noise to wake the dead.

We landed in a tangled heap at the bottom. I was lying face down; all I could see was carpet.

'Are you OK?' I turned my head to look at Prudence.

Instead, I saw a foot. A foot in a high-heeled silvery boot, resting on top of Sir Crispin ... *Oh, no*, I thought. *Oh, no!*

Diamond Pye pulled Prudence to her feet.

'A slippery little fish, aren't you?' she said, grasping Prudence by the elbow. 'First you wriggle out of a window, then you wriggle out of a cage. Let's put you in the Stuffing Room and see if you manage to wriggle out of that.'

'No!' Prudence shrank away from her, her face white and scared. 'No, please! Not there!'

'It's your own fault.' Diamond was impatient. 'I'm busy. I have no time for children right now.' Opening a door, she pushed Prudence in, then pointed her lollipop at me. 'You too.'

As I hesitated, she drew one of the chopsticks out of her hair, spinning it between her fingers. 'Hurry up, boy. I don't have all day.'

Prudence's eyes were fixed on the chopstick. 'George ... do as she says.'

'It's a chopstick,' I said. 'You can't hurt anything with a chopstick.'

'You can when it's sharpened and dipped in poison,' said Prudence. 'I've seen her kill a rat with that. The poor thing – it was horrible!'

Diamond laughed. I swallowed.

'It's very strong poison,' she told me. 'From a species of tree frog. It only takes a scratch. First your eyeballs melt, then your insides turn to soup and your brain begins to bubble out of your ears. Do you want to know what happens after that?'

I shook my head. Without a word, I followed Prudence .through the door.

The Stuffing Room must have once been a garage. It was dim, lit only by a little square window in the roof, until Diamond flipped a switch and fluorescent lights flickered on.

'Don't!' said Prudence, in a strangled voice. 'I don't want to see ...'

Diamond laughed. 'This is my favourite place,' she told me. 'Where I create my special pieces.'

Blinking in the glare of the lights, I looked around at the bare white walls and white-tiled floor. A row of gleaming metal instruments were laid out on a tray next to a marble slab. There were shelves of tall glass jars like the ones in the Sweet Shop – except they weren't full of sweets. Glass eyes, hundreds of them, all shapes and sizes and colours, stared back at me.

'Oh,' I said, the hairs prickling on the back of my neck. 'Is this where ...?'

'Yes,' said Prudence, in a very small voice.

I tried not to look at what was in the other glass jars. Bits of things, floating in murky liquid. I didn't want to look at the big white chest freezer in the corner, either. I really, really didn't want to know what was in it.

The far end of the room was screened off by a sort of giant plastic shower curtain.

'My *magnum opus*,' said Diamond, triumphantly. 'My greatest work so far. Why don't you have a look?'

'Don't!' said Prudence, again. 'Oh, please – don't!'

Something in her voice made me do it. I couldn't not. I pulled back the curtain.

A horse. A big grey horse. Its rider was in battle armour from head to toe, and pointing a spear at something long and scaly, coiled in fat loops on the ground. Gaping jaws bristled with teeth. Featherless wings, bat-skin and bone, stretched out like sails to either side.

I turned cold, my stomach knotting. *Mortifer*, I thought. *She's killed Mortifer.*

But that didn't make any sense. Not even Diamond could kill and stuff a basilisk in the time it had taken us to get out of the Trophy Room and down the stairs.

'What is it?'

'Can't you tell?' Diamond sounded annoyed. 'Saint George, of course. And the dragon.'

I looked at the 'dragon's' coils, and remembered the story of Mintzer and the stolen snake.

'That's Long Sally!'

'Mr Mintzer has his uses,' agreed Diamond. 'He had his revenge on the crocodile that bit off his hand – that's its head. The wings belonged to a wandering albatross. I plucked them myself. It's good, don't you think?'

'You shouldn't have done that to Long Sally,' was all I could think of to say. 'Or the crocodile. Or the poor albatross.'

Diamond laughed. 'Silly boy. How many dumb beasts get the chance to become a Work of Art? I have improved on Nature, and they were lucky to be a part of it. But is it enough to win the Golden Brain Spoon?'

'I shall not rest,' she declared, 'until the Spoon is mine and I am Taxidermist of the Year. But for that, I need perfection. I had little hope of finding a real dragon, then I heard rumours about the Squermington Wyrm. Now I've seen it, I must confess I am a little disappointed. I was hoping for something with legs. Never mind – it will have to do.'

'You'll never catch it,' I said. 'Never!'

'Oh, didn't I tell you?' Diamond bit into her lollipop with a splintering crunch. 'I already have. We threw some fried chicken into the pool house. The Wyrm went in after it. We've locked it in, safe and sound. I'll deal with it in the morning. This evening I have other plans. I am going to pay a little visit to Wormestall Farm. I have the strangest feeling that I'm going to like it there. Something tells me that there's some serious catching and bagging and stuffing to be done.'

There was no way out. As soon as Diamond had gone, I tried both doors – the one that led into the house and the big garage door – but neither of them budged. The skylight was too high to reach.

'Oh well,' I said, more cheerfully than I felt. 'We'll just have to play the Million Game.'

Once I had explained the only rule – keep counting, at a

steady pace, until something happens – Prudence started straight away. I started too, but I couldn't concentrate; I kept losing count. I'd drawn the curtain again, so we didn't have to look at St George and the dragon, but it didn't really work: the shadowy shapes behind the plastic sheet were somehow bigger and spookier than the real thing. I didn't want to upset Prudence by wondering it out loud, but I couldn't get the question out of my head: what, exactly, was inside St George's suit of armour?

It's just a dummy, I told myself. *Like Mum's mermaid. Or rags and newspaper, like that guy Dad made for Bonfire Night when I was six.*

At that moment there was a sudden loud thud, just above my head. Something had crash-landed on the roof.

Prudence gave a small, scared squeak. 'What's that?'

'It's all right,' I said. 'I think I know.'

There was a scraping sound as the skylight opened. I held my breath, hoping I was right. Something dangled through the gap. First a foot. Then a leg. Then a boy.

Lo dropped neatly through the skylight, landing on the horse's neck.

'Funny place to park a horse,' he said, patting it.

'It's Saint George,' I told him. 'And that's the dragon. Except Diamond's after a better one. She's got Mortifer!'

'We have to rescue him!' said Prudence. 'Quickly!'

Lo shook his head. 'He's safer where he is. The town's in an uproar over that little girl. There are search parties out looking for the Wyrm. They want it dead.'

'So does Diamond!' I pointed out.

'She won't do anything tonight,' said Prudence. 'She's going to Wormestall, remember? She hasn't given up on finding a proper dragon. We have to warn Mrs Lind.'

'If I stand on the horse,' said Lo, 'and you stand on my shoulders, do you think you could get through that skylight?'

We managed it, somehow. I couldn't leave Sir Crispin behind, so once Prudence was safely on the garage roof, I handed him up to her. Then it was my turn. It was like practising circus acrobatics. The ground seemed a long way away and I wobbled a lot, but I made it. Lo sprang up after me, in a sort of flying leap.

'How long,' he asked Prudence, 'until they realize you're gone?'

'Sometimes, when they shut me up, they forget about me for ages,' she said. 'It's usually Mump who comes, in the end. But George hit him over the head.'

'I had to,' I said. 'He was about to shoot Mortifer.'

'Saint George saves the day!' Lo grinned. 'Good man! I'll go on ahead. You two follow. Stick together,' he warned. 'And be careful. Do you see that?'

From the Stuffing Room roof, nearly at the top of High Holly Hill, you could see all the way down into the town. In Market Square we could see a crowd of people beneath the town clock.

'Don't they look tiny!' I said. 'What are they doing?'

They seemed to be forming a queue, like kids on a school trip. As we watched, the line began to move, past the Library and the One-Pound Shop and the Chinese takeaway, and through the SupaSava car park. It was coming our way, growing longer as it came. And it seemed to be on fire.

'They've lit torches.' Lo's face was grim. 'All the better for burning the Wyrm. And they're armed. Spades, forks, carving knives – you name it, they've got it. They're hunting blood. Can't you hear them?'

Kill the Wyrm! Kill the Wyrm! Death to the Wyrm! Kill ... Death ... Kill ...'

We could all hear it now. I shivered.

'You can smell it,' said Lo. 'All the anger and fear and hate. That mob is much more dangerous than any dragon or basilisk. It must be a thousand years since the people of Squermington rose up like this. The world changes, but people don't. It never ends well.'

Getting down from the roof wasn't too bad. There was a helpful tree and some bins to shorten the drop. Prudence went down the wall like a spider, landing without a sound.

'Sssh!' She put her finger to her lips as I clattered down beside her, and flipped open the top of a wheelie bin. 'Get in!'

'Are you joking? What for? It stinks.'

'Just get *in!* Diamond's coming!'

I stopped arguing and dived head first into the wheelie bin, curling myself into a ball as Prudence slammed the lid down on top of me and everything went dark. There was something soft in the bottom. Soft and very, very smelly. My ears and nose filled up with rotting stuff. I thought of the squishy things floating in Diamond's jars of formaldehyde and my stomach heaved. I began to feel panicky: nobody wants to be shut up in a wheelie bin with their own sick. I would have kicked the lid open and wriggled out into the fresh air, but just then I heard Diamond's voice, too close for comfort.

'Such a fuss,' she was saying, 'over a little bump on the head! Do stop groaning, Mr Mump – it's getting on my nerves. We'll take the van. We'll need it to bring the animals back. I've already put the sacks in the back. And plenty of rope and metal chains. I'm sure you can stop bleeding if you try. Knot this scarf around your forehead – like that. It will stop the blood from running into your eyes.' Through the mush in my ears, I heard her laugh. 'You and Mr Mintzer make a fine pair of pirates. Why are those people making so much noise?' she added. 'They're giving me a headache. What are they shouting about?'

'They're hunting the Wyrm,' explained Mintzer's voice. 'It stole a child. They're going after it.'

'Well, they can't have it,' said Diamond. 'It's mine. They can thank me when I've stuffed it. Perhaps we'll put it on display, in a nice glass case. There'll be a plaque, with my name on: "*Diamond Pye, Winner of the Golden Brain Spoon. Taxidermist of the Year, Stuffer Supreme and Saviour of Squermington.*" How about that?'

'Very pretty,' approved Mintzer. 'And no more than you deserve.'

'I am the best,' Diamond agreed. 'And soon people will know it.'

Footsteps crunched on gravel. Doors slammed. It was a tight fit in my bin, but I managed to wriggle the right way up. I used the top of my head to open the lid a little way. I could see Diamond in the driver's seat of the van, licking her lollipop, with Mintzer beside her. I turned my head and met Prudence's eyes, looking out of the bin next to mine.

In the house, the telephone was ringing.

'Nnnghh?' said Mump, answering it. 'Nnnghh! Nnnghh nnnghh nnnghh.'

'Hurry up, Mr Mump!' ordered Diamond, her long nails drumming on the steering wheel. 'Where are the keys? We haven't got all day! We want to get to the farm before it's too dark to see anything!'

Prudence and I ducked down, lowering our lids, as Mump shambled into view. Dark blood was oozing out from under his bandana and he seemed to be in a bit of a daze. The van's engine growled into life. Gravel sprayed as it jerked forward and out of the gates.

Prudence's lid flipped open and she scrambled out of her bin.

'Quick – we haven't got long. You reek of cat food,' she added.

'So do you.' I clambered out of the rubbish, raining little bits of potato peel. There was a damp teabag sticking to my cheek. 'Where's Lo?'

We looked, but he wasn't in any of the bins. He wasn't anywhere.

'He was there on the roof. Then he wasn't.' Prudence frowned. 'How did he get down?'

'Lo can look after himself,' I told her. 'Listen to the crowd!'

'To the woods! To the woods! Death to the Wyrm. Kill! Kill! Kill the Wyrm!'

The mob was pushing past the Pyes' gate, taking up the whole road as it twisted up the hill towards Wyvern Chase Woods, chanting in rhythm to the beat of a drum.

'Come on,' I said to Prudence. 'Let's join in. Nobody will notice us in among that lot. It's the safest place to be. We'll stick with them for a bit, then head off the other way to my house. We'll get to Wormestall faster on bikes. There's one you can borrow. It's a bit girly ...'

'That's OK,' said Prudence. 'I'm a girl. Or had you forgotten?'

To be honest, I had.

CHAPTER FOURTEEN

e wriggled our way right into the middle of the crowd, bodies pressing all around us, the heat from the torches stinging our cheeks. *'Death to the Wyrm! Death to the Wyrm!'* The drumbeat was like a heartbeat: it got under your skin and made your blood pulse. We even did a bit of shouting, to make it look as if we belonged.

There were people there I knew: Mum's hairdresser, the kind lady at the dentist's who gave me stickers when I was little, Harry's ex-boyfriend Danny who delivers pizzas on a scooter, Mr Mukherjee from the Star of India. They were nice people, people I liked, but it was as if they had all turned into zombies, their eyes and mouths black holes of hate. I didn't want to think about what would happen if they got all the way through Wyvern Chase Woods and turned right – towards Wormestall Farm. They were hungry for a kill. If they found Grissel, nothing would stop them finishing what St George had started more than a thousand years ago. They wouldn't care that she wasn't the Squermington Wyrm. They would chop her into pieces anyway. Something had to be done. But first, something had to be done about Diamond.

I grabbed Prudence's arm. There *was* Diamond!

The blare of the van's horn had got mixed up with all the other sounds, but now I saw the van itself, a little way ahead of us, trapped in the crush of marchers. Diamond could honk her horn all she liked; there was nothing she could do. As the van crawled along at walking pace, someone jumped up onto the bonnet.

'Death to the Wyrm!' he shouted, louder than all the rest. I recognized him from the newspaper. It was Spike Hardman, Little Lily Lamprey's neighbour.

'Kill the Wyrm!' the crowd roared back.

'Now!' I hissed in Prudence's ear, pulling her down a side street. We stayed pressed up against a wall until the tail end of the mob had passed us.

'Come on,' I said. 'This way.'

Squermington was like a ghost town, the streets deserted. Everybody was off on the Great Wyrm Hunt. When we got to my house, we could see the TV through the front window. Frank was still on the sofa, watching something about penguins. Then the light snapped on and Mum moved forwards to draw the curtains. I ducked out of sight.

'Round the back,' I whispered to Prudence. 'The bikes are in the shed.'

We lost quite a lot of time because we had to pump up

the tyres on the Princess PrettyPants bike. To make as little noise as possible, we carried both bikes across the garden and out of the back gate. Nobody saw. Nobody heard.

Now all we had to do was get to Wormestall – before the Wyrm Hunters and before Diamond Pye.

By the time we reached the farm, we were both red in the face and panting. We had cycled through the darkening streets as if all the Hounds of Hell were snapping at our back wheels. I would rather have had the Hounds of Hell than Diamond. Compared with her, they were probably quite cuddly.

Big Nigel wasn't in his field. I hoped that meant that Lo had come back and hidden him somewhere safe. There was just a rabbit, nibbling grass in the twilight. I stared at it. Its tail was tinged with green.

'The stone rabbit! Look – it's been de-petrified!'

At the sound of my voice, the rabbit sat up, ears quivering, then flicked its green tail and bounded away. We never saw where it went.

We'd both heard the sound we had been dreading: the growl of an engine not far behind us.

In the kitchen, the now familiar smell of boiled leaves and cat litter hung in the air. Mrs Lind was sitting at the table, dipping a paintbrush into a steaming bowl of green sludge. In front of her, on a sheet of old newspaper, was a stone cat. It had one leg pointing up in the air and a surprised expression on its face.

'Excellent news,' said Mrs Lind. 'The ointment's working at last! Did you see the rabbit?'

I nodded. 'But don't de-petrify anything else. Not yet.' The cat was safer staying stone while Diamond was around. 'Prudence's stepmother's on her way. She'll be here any minute!'

'Lo told me.' Mrs Lind put down her paintbrush. 'He took Big Nigel up to the barn, out of sight, and shut Tail-biter up in one of the bedrooms. Then he disappeared. I don't know where he's gone.'

'What about Dido?' asked Prudence. We all looked at the dodo, dozing in her dog bed. 'We should hide her.'

Mrs Lind shook her head. 'She won't budge. One of those eggs is pipping. Whatever's inside is tapping on the shell, getting ready to hatch. Dido won't leave it.'

'There isn't time, anyway.' I said. 'Listen.'

Diamond had arrived.

She didn't bother with the doorbell. She just walked right in, Mump and Mintzer at her heels. When she saw Prudence and me, she frowned. Then she saw Dido.

'Fancy that!' she said, her mouth curling into a crocodile smile. 'A real live dodo!'

'I'd let her be, if I were you,' warned Mrs Lind, as Dido hissed and clicked her beak. 'She can be snappy.'

'Not when she's stuffed,' promised Diamond.

'You can't stuff Dido,' Mrs Lind said, firmly. 'She is the

last of her kind.'

'All the more reason to stuff her,' said Diamond. 'Then she'll last for ever. I'll have *that*.' She pointed at Mingus, curled up on Mrs Lind's hat. 'And what's *this*?' Diving under the table, she fished the Ping Feng piglet out of its box. 'A living freak,' she breathed, unwrapping it from its blanket and holding it up in the air. The piglet squealed and wriggled. 'Two heads and not a stitch, not a seam anywhere: perfect! Nobody will believe it; they will think it is my own creation. I shall win the Golden Brain Spoon again and again and again!'

'No!' cried Prudence. 'Leave it alone!'

Diamond just laughed. 'Sorry!' she said. 'Finders stuffers! Mr Mump! Where's the sack?'

'Unnghh?' said Mump. He was bending over the hob, sniffing the De-petrifaction Ointment. 'Mmmnghh,' he said. 'Jam.' He dipped a finger into the green gunge, and popped it in his mouth. 'Jam.'

'Oh dear,' said Mrs Lind. 'You probably didn't want to do that.'

'We're not here to eat jam, Mr Mump!' snapped Diamond. 'Mr Mintzer! Bag that pig thing!'

'Right away, Mrs Pye.' Mintzer took the squirming piglet by the scruff of one of its necks and dropped it into a sack

'And that dodo!' ordered Diamond. 'Keep an eye on the old lady and those pesky sprats. I'm going to have a look around. They're hiding something more from us, I'm sure of it.'

Her silver heels click-clacked on the flagstones, out of the kitchen and across the hall to the door.

Mintzer was grinning at Dido.

'Here, pretty birdie,' he crooned, opening up another sack. 'Come and be stuffed.'

Maybe it was the sack she didn't like the look of. Maybe it was Mintzer's lilac spotted bow-tie. Maybe she just didn't like being called birdie. Anyway, before Mintzer could throw himself on *her*, Dido threw herself at *him*. There was a flurry of feathers and squawking and not very nice language, then Mintzer's foot lashed out. Dido flew through the air, in the way that dodos shouldn't, landing with a *flump* in the sink. Mrs Lind scooped her up, tucking her under one arm.

'That's no way to treat a very rare bird,' she told Mintzer, fiercely.

'The bird started it,' he sneered. 'Hand it over, old woman.'

I felt a rush of anger fizz through me, like an electric current. I planted myself between Mintzer and Mrs Lind.

'Leave her alone!'

Mintzer breathed on his hook, polishing it with his hanky. 'Mr Mump!' he called. 'Get rid of this irritating brat! I don't care what you do with it."

'NNNNNGGGGHHHH!' said Mump.

We all turned and looked at him in surprise. He had suddenly folded up, clutching his stomach.

'Nnghh!' he groaned again. 'Nnnghh! Bad jam!

Nnnghh! Toilet!'

'Upstairs,' I told him. 'Turn right. Second left.'

Still holding his stomach, Mump staggered out of the kitchen. We could hear his footsteps reach the top of the stairs and stumble down the corridor. Then we heard the door slam as he shut himself in the bathroom.

I dodged as Mintzer sliced the air with his hook.

'Give me the bird,' he snarled. 'Or I'll poke your eyeballs out!'

At that moment the slashing hook caught Mrs Lind's hat, knocking the brim. Several walnuts and a kiwi fruit landed on the floor and went rolling into corners. Mingus, who had been comfortably asleep, woke up and found someone had been messing with his fruit.

Chittering with rage, he made a leap for the top of the dresser, where he deployed his secret weapon. He pointed his bottom at Mintzer and PSSSSSHT! We were all choking and spluttering in a cloud of something that made De-petrifaction Ointment smell like a bunch of roses.

Somehow, in the mad rush for the door, Mintzer blundered into Prudence, who crashed into Mrs Lind, who bumped into me. Losing my balance, I teetered backwards, and put my foot in Dido's dog bed.

There was a horrible sound of splintering eggshell.

Oh no! I thought. *What have I done?* Every single one of those eggs was incredibly rare and special and beyond price. But nobody had noticed. They were all heading for the stableyard, gasping for fresh air. Dido, squawking loudly, was still tucked under Mrs Lind's arm.

Holding my nose, my eyes streaming from the Mingus Explosion, I bent down to check the damage. Only one egg seemed to have cracked. There was nothing I could do about it now. I would just have to own up and hope that Mrs Lind would forgive me in the end, even if Dido didn't.

I was about to hurry after the others when I heard something. A *pip-pip-pip* sound. I blinked hard, staring at the crack. I wasn't imagining it. *Pip-pip-pip*. It was more than a crack now. The pipping stopped. Now there was a different noise.

Weep-weep-weep.

I stared even harder.

And the egg stared back.

Just for a moment, I forgot about Diamond and Mintzer and the danger the farm was in. I felt a burst of excitement, like a firework going off in my stomach. A brand-new baby had just taken its first look at the world, and the first thing it saw was me. But a brand-new baby what?

Then the excitement fizzled away. It didn't matter what it was. It was just one more thing that had to be kept out of Diamond's sight. If I didn't hide it, and quickly, the poor little thing would get stuffed before it had even scrambled out of its egg.

Weep-weep-weep.

It was calling to me.

'Not now,' I told it. 'I'm really sorry. Please understand. I haven't got time. I have to look after Prudence and Mrs

Lind, and save the other animals. Seriously, it's a dangerous world out here. I'm going to wrap you up' – I reached for a tea towel – 'and put you somewhere safe.' I opened the bread bin. 'Just for now. I'll come and get you when it's safe. Until I do – please, please, stay in your egg!'

As I raced across the hall, following the others, I could just hear Mump's shouts from upstairs.

'Nnnnghh! Thinggghh!'

Mump had met the kraken. One down. Two to go.

CHAPTER FIFTEEN

Out in the yard, things weren't going well. In the middle of a whirling cloud of dodo feathers, Mintzer and Mrs Lind were having a fight. Mintzer was armed with his hook. Mrs Lind was armed with Dido, whose great curved beak snapped and clicked and tried to tear lumps out of any part of Mintzer within reach. The stable doors all stood open except for the last one – Grissel's. Prudence was standing in front of it, with a stormy look on her face and her arms folded.

'Get out of my way,' ordered Diamond.

'No,' said Prudence. 'I won't.'

'You always were as stubborn as a donkey,' complained Diamond. 'Do you know what happened to the last donkey I met? I made it into a rocking horse. Other people have pretty little daughters who do as they're told. Why did I end up with you?'

'Because you married my father,' said Prudence. 'You

didn't have to. I wish you hadn't.'

'Ungrateful girl!' Diamond stamped her foot, catching the high silver heel in the cobblestones and nearly losing her balance. 'After I've fed you, clothed you, cared for you ...'

'You made Mr Mump do all that,' said Prudence. 'All you did was stuff my dog.'

'Your last chance,' said Diamond. 'I'll count to five. And if you're *still* in my way ...' Reaching behind her head, she pulled a chopstick out of her hair. 'One. Two ...'

'No!' I went to stand beside Prudence. 'Leave her alone!'

Diamond shrugged, spinning the chopstick between her fingers. 'Suit yourself. There's enough poison on this to kill a herd of elephants. Two annoying children won't be a problem. Where was I? Two. Three. Four ...'

'*Got* you!' said Mintzer.

The fight was over. He had rammed Mrs Lind's hat down over her eyes, so she couldn't see. And because she was holding Dodo, she couldn't move her arms either.

'And *you*,' he added, throwing a sack over Dido and tying it tightly around her neck. 'I've bagged your bird, Mrs Pye. And the old lady, too.'

'Excellent work, Mr Mintzer,' said Diamond. 'Put them in the van.'

Mintzer gripped Mrs Lind's wrists, dragging her towards the back of the van. He opened it up with a flick of his hook and then went suddenly still. Very, very still.

'George. Prue. Close your eyes.' Lo stepped out from behind the van. 'Close your eyes *now*. Do *not* open them.'

We did as he said, although it's really, really hard to keep your eyes shut when something's happening but you don't know what.

I heard Mrs Lind say, 'It's *you*! You're back! I know it's you – I can smell chicken korma! All the trouble you've caused, you bad boy! We've missed you.'

Then I understood.

Mortifer, at long last, had come home.

Groping around in my pocket for Diamond's mirrored sunglasses. I put them on, then risked opening my eyes. Prudence had had the same idea. We looked at our reflections in each other's eyes, then we looked at Mintzer. He was pale and petrified, frozen in stone.

'A hardened criminal,' said Lo.

Carefully, sideways, I sneaked a glance at Mortifer from behind my shades. He seemed pleased to be home, rubbing up against Mrs Lind, looping his fat copper coils around her. Stretched out, he'd have reached the length of a swimming pool: a giant serpent, with a beaked nose and mane of golden feathers.

'How did you get him in the van?' I demanded.

'Easy,' said Lo. 'I hid the keys. While the big fellow was blundering about looking for them, I unpicked the lock on the shed. The telephone rang, which gave me couple of extra minutes. I'd already popped into the Star of India, just in case. Mortifer can't resist a chicken korma. All I had to do was put it in the back of the van.'

'Everything will be all right,' said Mrs Lind happily. 'Now that Mortifer's back.'

She spoke too soon.

'I knew it!' Diamond's voice rang out, triumphant. '*That's* what I was looking for!'

Grissel had been dozing in front of *Celebrity SuperChef*. As Diamond flung open the stable doors and stepped inside, high heels crunching on the carpet of stones, she opened her one eye.

Diamond brandished her lollipop excitedly. 'It won't be easy!' she said. 'The creature looks half-dead. Broken down. Bits of it are missing. Only the best taxidermist in the world could make it look new again. Only *me*!'

It's never a good idea barging in on a dragon empty-handed. Smoke drifted from the back of the stable. Pebbles rattled.

'Grissel's not an *it*. She's a she,' I said. 'And I wouldn't wave that lollipop around, if I were you. She'll smell the sugar.'

Some people never listen.

Maybe it was just the lollipop Grissel was after. Maybe not. It was a long time since she had tasted human meat. Perhaps she fancied a change. Who knows? It happened very quickly, and might have been quite straightforward, in a dragon-eats-evil-stepmother sort of way, if it hadn't been for Diamond's chopsticks. The points must have stuck, like fish hooks, inside Grissel's jaw. Confused, the dragon swung her head from side to side, trying to either swallow what she had in her mouth or spit it out. Prudence and I backed away as sparks jetted from her flaring nostrils. Diamond's legs, in her high silver boots, were kicking furiously. Her shouts came out muffled, but I could hear enough: mostly about what she was going to do to Grissel and Mortifer and the rest of us if we didn't hurry up and save her.

'Why can I smell fireworks?' enquired Mrs Lind from under her hat. Lo had rescued Dido, but Mrs Lind was stuck. Mintzer's stone fingers still clutched her arm. 'What's going on?'

'Nothing to worry about,' said Lo. 'Grissel's found herself a human lollipop. The lollipop's making a fuss.'

At that moment, Grissel, getting panicky, burst out of her stable and took to the air. We watched her climb higher and higher, zigzagging and circling, straining with her damaged wing.

'She's heading for the duck pond,' said Lo. 'Come on.'

Leaving Mrs Lind behind, we raced through the vegetable garden and the orchard and down the slope to the pond. We got there just as Grissel dived. She buzzed low over my ichthyosaur-training tree and, with a cracking of twigs and a furious yell, Diamond and her chopsticks came free and landed in the branches. Grissel hovered for a moment, then soared away.

'Just you wait!' Diamond yelled, wringing dragon spit out of her hair. 'I'll stuff every living thing in this place! I'll put the whole lot of you in glass cases! Yes, *you* – and *you*!'

She had seen Donald and Jemima, peering out from behind the bushes to see what the fuss was about. Then she pointed straight at Prudence and me. 'And you and you!'

Beside me, Prudence was trembling. 'She's coming for us! She's so angry ... George, she means what she says!'

'Don't panic.' I sounded calmer than I felt. An idea was flapping about in my head. I looked at the silver boots dangling over the water, glinting in the very last rays of sunlight. Glinting like fish scales. I wasn't sure whether it was a totally brilliant idea, or an absolutely catastrophic one. I wasn't even sure if it would work. I took a deep breath. And whistled.

Nothing happened, except that Prudence and Lo both turned their heads to stare at me as if I'd gone mad.

Diamond was pulling herself along the branch. Soon she would be out of reach. Was it my imagination or did the water ripple? I whistled again.

'There'll be nothing left!' shrieked Diamond. 'I'll catch you and bag you and—'

A fin broke the surface.

My beautiful, intelligent, ever-so-well-trained ichthyosaur.

Leaping into the air, as graceful as any dolphin, deadlier than any killer whale, it opened its jaws to claim its reward.

'*STUFF YOU ...*'

For an instant in time, the words hung in the early evening air.

Then everything went quiet.

Prudence and I walked back to the house, leaving Lo to wait and see what, if anything, floated to the surface of the pond. Neither of us spoke. We didn't know what to say.

Mrs Lind was sitting on the basilisk's coils, still locked in Mintzer's stone grip, with Mortifer's feathered head resting in her lap. Blindfolded by her hat, she cocked her head when she heard our footsteps.

'What happened?' she asked.

'The ichthyosaur happened,' I told her. 'It won't need feeding tonight.'

'That will save on fish,' said Mrs Lind, practically. 'What about Grissel?'

Where was Grissel? I looked up at the sky. A long, long, long way up, a black dot was circling.

'The chopsticks!' Prudence's hand flew to her mouth. 'They're dipped in deadly tree frog juice. Oh, no ...' Her eyes had filled with tears.

'You can't poison a dragon. It doesn't work. The poison burns up inside them,' said Mrs Lind. 'But there are sometimes side effects. Can you see her? What's she doing?'

I peered upwards. 'I *think* she's just looped the loop ...'

'It won't do,' said Mrs Lind. 'We can't have a grown dragon turning cartwheels up there. She'll be chasing aeroplanes next. Lo will have to go and get her.'

I was about to say I didn't quite see *how* when Lo appeared holding one high-heeled silver boot.

'I reckon the ichthyosaur must have swallowed the other one,' he said. 'What are you all looking so serious about?'

'It's Grissel,' I told him. 'She's up there, out of her head on frog juice.'

We all looked up, except for Mrs Lind, who couldn't. The dot in the sky was behaving weirdly: stopping and starting and doing mad zigzags, like flies do when you spray them with fly poison.

'It's not safe,' said Mrs Lind. 'You'll have to go after her, Lo.'

High up, a low hum sounded. Lights tracked across the sky. An aeroplane. The black dot that was Grissel hung motionless for a moment, then shot after it.

'She's catching up,' I said.

'Oh, do hurry!' begged Mrs Lind.

'It's cold up there, you know,' grumbled Lo. 'And, unlike the ichthyosaur, I haven't had any supper. But I suppose I haven't any choice. I wouldn't say no to a cup of hot chocolate when I get back, if anybody felt like making one.'

He disappeared inside. A moment or two later, we saw his face at an upstairs window. Swinging his leg over the sill, he pulled himself up onto the roof.

Prudence grabbed my arm. '*Look*!'

For the first time since I had known him, Lo shrugged off his heavy hooded jacket. He twitched his shoulders. Left. Right. Both together. Then he did something I wasn't expecting.

He stretched out his wings.

CHAPTER SIXTEEN

Black feathers. They were always a few of them floating around Wormestall, drifting in corners, rocking in the breeze. I'd sometimes wondered if Lo had been cooking crows. I'd never imagined this.

'The A-word,' I breathed, watching him dive upwards into thin air until he was just a full stop on a page of sky. '*That's* what the A stands for! He's an A—'

'Amazingly-useful-person-to-have-around-at-a-time-like-this,' said Mrs Lind. 'He'll bring her back. He has a way with dragons.'

She was right. They spiralled downwards out of space, growing bigger and bigger. Talons scraped on stone as Grissel skidded on the cobbles. A moment later there was a thud, and a rude word, and Lo was on the roof. Black wings folded with a whisper of feathers.

'She's frothing at the mouth.' Prudence stroked Grissel's neck. 'The chopsticks hurt her. And the poison must taste horrible. Shouldn't we give her a drink of water?'

'Never give dragons water,' said Mrs Lind. 'It makes them fizz. She'd prefer ice cream. I don't like this horrid man holding my hand. Lo, can you set me free?'

'We'll have to break him,' said Lo, sliding feet first through the upstairs window. 'I'll need tools.'

A few minutes later he came out of the house, swinging a toolbox.

'You're not the only one who's stuck,' he told Mrs Lind. 'The other man – the big fellow. The kraken's roped him to the toilet and won't let go.'

Mump. I'd forgotten all about him.

'Oh, poor Mump!' said Prudence. 'We should rescue him.'

'And then what?' enquired Lo. 'We can't just let him go. He's seen too much. He'll talk.'

Prudence shook her head. 'Not Mump. He doesn't really *do* talking. He won't say anything if I tell him not to. He's good at doing what he's told. And ... I need him.' She bit her lip. 'I don't want to live in that house all by myself. It's full of dead things. Mump's all I have left.'

Prudence settled Grissel back into her stable while Lo chipped away at Mintzer's fingers with a chisel. Mortifer was dozing snake-style, ruby eyes open. Lo didn't seem worried about avoiding them. I guessed that getting petrified wasn't something that happened to his sort.

It was left to me to call off the kraken, so I headed to the freezer for fish fingers. The kraken would do pretty much anything for a fish finger. It was Prudence who had found this out. She didn't enjoy watching goldfish being nibbled to death any more than I did, so she had gone shopping in Eezy-Freezy Foods on her way to Wormestall one day and done some experimenting.

Dido was in the kitchen, fussing over her eggs. She tapped each one in turn with her beak, almost as if she was counting them, then cocked her head to one side, listening. A muffled *weep-weep-weep* came from the direction of the bread bin. There were fragments of eggshell on the floor. Dido stared at them, very hard, then glared at me.

'All right,' I owned up. 'It was me. I trod on it. But it was hatching anyway. You can have it back now.'

I lifted the egg out of the bread bin and put it carefully back in the dog bed. Through the hole in the eggshell, the amber eye fixed on mine and wouldn't let go.

'There's your baby,' I told Dido. 'Look after it.' And I hurried away to rescue Mump.

It took six fish fingers to get the kraken back in the bath. Mump slid off the toilet seat, crumpling up in a heap on the floor, with his hands over his face, making little '*nnghh nnghh*' moaning sounds. I patted him on the shoulder. I hadn't forgotten my own first meeting with the kraken.

'It's safe now,' I told him. 'Come downstairs. Things have been happening while you were ... busy. Prudence will explain. But you might want to pull your trousers up.'

In the kitchen, Mrs Lind was giving the Ping Feng piglet its bottle. There was a red circle around her wrist where Mintzer's stone fingers had squeezed her. Prudence was spooning ice cream into a bucket to give to Grissel, while Lo sprawled on a chair with his feet on the table, eating a banana.

'Guess what!' said Prudence, when she saw me. 'One of Dido's eggs is hatching. It's an Egg Surprise – we don't know what's in it!'

Mrs Lind tut-tutted over Mump's pale face and bloodstained bandana.

'Alicorn,' she said, passing me the piglet and reaching for the first aid box. 'For the bleeding. Prue, put some of that ice cream in a bowl for Mr Mump. It's the best thing, after a Nasty Experience.'

Twenty minutes later, Mump had had his face washed, his bandage changed, and a large bowl of ice cream. He sat stroking Next Door's Stone Cat and looking much more cheerful.

'It's going to be just you and me, now,' Prudence told him. 'It'll feel a bit odd to begin with, I expect, but it's all going to work out fine. We'll have fun. And ice cream, whenever we want. And if you promise not to say a *word*, not a word to *anybody* about Wormestall and what you've seen here, then Mrs Lind will make Smelly Betty better.'

'Bring her to see me tomorrow,' said Mrs Lind. 'We'll have a Grand De-petrifaction Day.'

It was late. Mum was going to be cross. Prudence didn't have anyone left to be cross with her. That was a good thing, obviously – and certainly better than being locked in a cage – but I thought it might feel a bit lonely.

'If you like,' I told her, 'you can sleep over at my house. Mum won't mind. We'll tell her Diamond's ... had an accident. Then she can't say no.'

We didn't want to leave until the Whatever-It-Was had come out of its egg, but Mrs Lind said that might take ages.

'A big egg like that has a tough shell,' she explained. 'It's hard work, chipping your way out. Dido will help. She's had plenty of practice. She hatched out Donald and Jemima, you know, as well as all those archaeopteryx. Come back tomorrow. It's been a long day.'

So Prudence and I set off on our bikes, leaving Mump to eat another bowl of ice cream before driving home in the van.

'Death to the Wyrm. Kill the Wyrm. Kill! Death! Kill!'

Prudence and I heard it at the same time, and braked. We could see the light from the blazing torches, flickering between the trees.

I had forgotten all about the Great Wyrm Hunt. They must have been searching the woods, and not found anything. Now they came spilling out on to the lane, still shouting and waving their weapons. They wanted blood. And they were much, much too close to Wormestall.

'Death to the Wyrm,' shouted the man in front. It was

Spike Hardman, their leader. 'You two shouldn't be out on your own. It's not safe. Don't you know there's a dangerous Wyrm about?'

'Not around here,' I said. 'Haven't you heard? It's been seen.'

'Where?' demanded Spike.

'*Kill it! Kill it!*' growled the mob behind him.

'That way.' I pointed down a turning that would take them in the opposite direction from Wormestall. There was a signpost: '*Lower Downton 4 km*'. It would take them a while, there and back. 'Somebody *definitely* saw it in Lower Downton very recently. It's still there. You had better hurry, or you'll miss it.'

'Death to the Wyrm!' shouted Spike, raising his garden fork above his head.

'Kill it! Kill it!' shouted his loyal followers, and they went pouring down the lane to Lower Downton.

'That got rid of them,' I said, with relief.

'Yes, for *now*,' said Prudence. 'But they'll be back when they don't find anything at Lower Downton. They'll keep coming back, and sooner or later they'll get as far as Wormestall. And then what?'

Mrs Lind was right: it had been a long day. I wanted to be at home, in my pyjamas on the sofa, having the usual arguments with Frank about who watched what on TV.

'We'll think of something,' I told Prudence. I hoped I was right.

We coasted down High Holly Hill on our bikes. Prudence's house was in darkness. I shivered as we passed it, remembering the Stuffing Room and wondering what would have happened if Lo hadn't come to our rescue.

We took the short cut, through the bus station, past the recycling bins and the Public Toilets.

Just outside the Ladies, Prudence stopped.

'Can't you wait?' I complained. 'We're nearly home. Anyway, look.' I pointed at the sign: 'Closed Until Further Notice.'

'I didn't stop for *that*,' said Prue. 'I know they're shut. So, why's there somebody in there? Listen!'

'Kill the Wyrm. Kill the Wyrm. Death to the Wyrm. Death to the Wyrm.'

'It's a Wyrm Hunter,' I said. 'They must have got left behind.' But there was something not quite right. This wasn't the bloodthirsty chant of the mob.

When I was very little, my gran used to sing me nursery rhymes.

'I know that tune. It's "Three Blind Mice",' I said, surprised. 'Hey, what are you doing?'

Prudence had scrambled up on top of the recycling bins. 'That's not a Wyrm Hunter! I'm going to see.'

The window was high and narrow, and only open a crack. Prudence reached an arm through the gap and felt for the catch, then slipped through. 'Aren't you coming?'

Reluctantly, I followed.

Prudence was balanced on a washbasin. She put her finger

— page 198 —

to her lips. 'Listen.'

The tune had changed to 'Twinkle Twinkle, Little Star'. Whoever it was, they only knew the words to the first two lines.

'Bluh-bluh, bluh-bluh, bluh-bluh-bluh.'

Prudence slid down from the washbasin. I was doing the same when my foot hit the hot tap. Water gushed and gurgled. The *bluh-bluhs* stopped.

'Is that my mum?' The voice came from one of the cubicles. 'Because I'd like to go home now.'

Prudence met my eyes, then knocked on the cubicle door.

'Hello – are you all right?'

'No,' said the voice. It sounded sniffy, as if its owner might be going to cry. 'I've eaten all the sweets *and* the biscuits and I've finished the cola and my tummy hurts and I'm all *wrong*.'

'Why don't you open the door?' suggested Prudence.

There was a lot of rustling, then somebody fumbled with the lock and the door swung open. Standing in a sea of sweet wrappers was a little girl with a round face and a runny nose, holding a floppy yellow elephant. There was a load of graffiti on the walls, mostly scribbled by school kids. Ryan 4 Amy, Katie-loves-Ben sort of stuff. Some of it must have been there for years – and some of it, in big red crayon letters, looked very new.

'Hey, have you been drawing on the walls?' I asked the little girl, sternly.

The letters were all different sizes, with the capitals in all the wrong places:

LiLy4sA ntA

LiLy LUV s cHok LiT

Is your name Lily Lamprey, by any chance?' asked Prudence, thoughtfully.

Lily nodded. 'And I don't love chocolate anymore. It just pretends to be nice. Then it gives you a tummy-ouch.'

I looked at the sweet wrappers all around her. 'How long have you been in here?'

'Ages. Since I ran away. You have to take stuff when you run away. I know that. I'm not *stupid*. So I took lots to eat, and my colouring pencils, and Yellow Elly.'

'What did you want to run away for?'

Lily gave a long, wet, bubbly sniff. 'They were mean to me.'

Prudence handed her some toilet roll for her nose. 'I know what it feels like when people are horrid to you. What did they do to you, Lily?'

'They wouldn't buy me Princess PrettyPants Party Palace,' complained Lily, and blew a big hole in the toilet paper. 'They said I had to wait till my birthday. And that's not for ages.'

'Is that all?' I stared at her. 'I thought it was going to be something bad – like they gave your puppy away, or fed you on slugs or something. Do you realize the whole town's been out looking for you? An innocent creature was nearly cut into a thousand pieces – all because of you!'

'I was going back,' said Lily, looking sulky. 'The sweets were all gone and I'd eaten all the biscuits. Even the ginger ones, and I don't like them. And I was bored of colouring in, and Yellow Elly's not much fun. I wanted to go home, but the door was stuck.'

'How did you get in to begin with?' asked Prudence.

Lily shrugged. 'There was a lady cleaning. She wasn't looking. And she was listening to music, so she didn't hear me. I shut the door, and sat on my feet so she couldn't see. Then she went away.'

'Well, if you ask me you're very silly and you deserve to be locked in a toilet.' I was tired and hungry, and not in the mood for whiny little kids. 'It would serve you right if we left you here.'

'We can't,' said Prudence. She looked at me. 'Don't you see? As soon as people find out Lily's safe, the Wyrm Hunt will be called off. We have to get her home as soon as possible.'

'Good luck getting her through that window,' I said. 'After all that chocolate!'

We did get Lily through the window, although we had to squash her a bit and she squealed louder than both ends of a Ping Feng put together.

'You can shut up now,' said Prudence, helping her down from the recycling bins. 'We're going to take you home. Where do you live?'

'Number one four,' said Lily. 'With a red door.' But she

didn't know which road, so that didn't help much.

'They put her address in the newspaper,' I remembered. 'It'll be in here somewhere.' I began pulling papers out of the recycling bins.

It didn't take long to find it. Lily stopped crying when she saw her photo in the paper.

'I'm a silly-ebrity!' she said, importantly.

'Don't get big-headed,' I told her. 'Loads of stupid people get their faces in the newspapers. You live in Blackberry Terrace. I know where that is – it's not far.'

Lily's gran was the only person at home. Everyone else was on the Wyrm Hunt.

'Our little princess!' she said, hugging Lily over and over again.

'If you squeeze me like that,' said her little princess, 'I'm going to be sick.'

Telephone calls were made, and the Wyrm Hunt was called off.

'You can't leave until they get here,' Lily's gran told us. 'Everybody wants to say thank you.' She made us cheese on toast while we waited, so it could have been worse.

When the Hunters got back, they all wanted to kiss and hug Lily, and then they all wanted to kiss and hug us. It can be very hard work being thanked. After a while, you wish people would stop.

Lily's dad said we deserved a reward. He took a wad of cash out of his wallet and started peeling off £20 notes.

'We can never repay you for finding our princess,' he told us. 'But here's a hundred pounds each.'

I had never held £100 before. I said Thank You Very Much, and hoped that Lily never told him I'd threatened to leave her locked in the toilet.

The police arrived and wanted to ask us questions, then a man from the News arrived and took pictures of us and asked more questions. We must have been yawning a lot by then, because somebody said, 'They're dead tired, those two. It's time somebody took them home.'

It was the Washing Machine Fix-it Man, who turned out to be Lily's uncle. As he knew where I lived, he said he'd take us in his van.

'How's your lovely mum?' the Fix-it Man asked me as he drove us home. He's been to our house so many times, he knows us quite well.

'Washing machine's broken again,' I told him.

'Not surprised,' he said. 'It belongs in a museum, that thing. Time she got a new one. I've got a nice one in the back of the van she could have. Nearly new – hardly been used. Seeing as it's your mum, I could let her have it for a hundred.'

'I don't think she's got a hundred pounds.' Then my head filled up with a thought. 'But ... *I* have.'

The Fix-it Man raised his eyebrows. 'Your reward money? Are you sure?'

Was I sure? I thought of all the things I could do with a hundred pounds. Then I thought of Mum standing on one leg in our flooded kitchen, looking tired and sad and Dad-less. I didn't need the money. I had my Wormestall wages. And I'd got my bike back, so the Emergency Bike Fund didn't matter anymore.

'Yes,' I said, before I could change my mind. 'Yes, I'm sure.' I didn't really deserve that money anyway. It was Prudence who had found Lily.

'Tell you what,' said the Fix-It Man. 'I'll knock twenty off the price. Call it eighty. And I'll install it for free. I can do it tomorrow, if you like.'

'Tomorrow would be perfect,' I said. I had just remembered Mum's birthday.

Mum was furious when we got home.

'Look at the time! I've been worried sick! I rang Prue's house hours ago to see if you were there!'

So that was the phone call Mump took. The one that gave Lo time to get Mortifer into the van.

'I thought you'd been eaten by that terrible Wyrm!' Mum sounded as if she really minded, which was nice.

'Don't be silly,' I said. 'There's no such thing as the Squermington Wyrm. Haven't you heard?'

Then the Fix-it Man told her about us finding Lily, and after that she had to stop being cross. Frank didn't believe us.

'Poppycock,' she said. 'You're making it up.'

But Harry turned on the local news and there were our pictures on TV. We were celebrities. Mum, Harry and Frank sat in a row on the sofa and stared, with their mouths hanging open.

'I'll be off, then.' The Fix-it Man gave me a wink as he was leaving, and mouthed the word 'tomorrow'.

When the news was over, Mum told Prudence she looked just like her mum.

'Same hair,' she said. 'And the same eyebrows.'

'I know.' Prudence sighed. 'They meet in the middle when I frown. At school, they say I'm a werewolf.'

'It would be good if you were,' I said. 'You could eat Miss Thripps. Mum, can Prudence sleep over? Her stepmother's ... not very well.'

'I don't see why not,' agreed Mum. 'I'll have to ring up, just to make sure.'

We heard her explaining everything over the phone.

'That's all sorted out,' she told us, when she had said goodbye. 'I talked to a very nice man. He didn't say much. Just *nngghh*.'

The next morning, Mum had a birthday breakfast. It was exactly the same as every-other-day breakfast, except that we took it up to her in bed, along with her presents. Prudence had rushed out with her reward money and bought all the jelly babies in the Sweet Shop. Mum loves jelly babies. Mrs Filling had been so surprised, she had even let Prudence take the big glass jar to bring them home in.

Harry's present was a pair of sparkly earrings and bubble bath in a bottle shaped like a mermaid.

'To make up for the one in the window,' she explained. 'I know you miss it.'

Frank gave her a very small pot with a meat-eating plant in it.

'Isn't it sweet? When it grows up, we can teach it to eat flies,' said Frank, helping herself to a handful of jelly babies. 'It'll be useful. Where's your present, George? I bet you haven't got one. You forgot. You're *hopeless*.'

'I didn't forget, actually. It's coming by Special Delivery,' I said, grandly. 'You'll see.'

'Yeah, right,' said Frank, but she couldn't be too rude because her ankle still hurt and she needed me to take care of Sir Crispin. (I didn't tell her he had been turned into stone. She thought he was safely at home. Why spoil her day?)

Mum was in the bath when the Fix-it Man arrived with the washing machine. Frank's face was worth every penny of eighty pounds. We couldn't wrap it up because it was too big, so we tied a bright red ribbon around it and used up a whole bottle of Harry's nail polish writing 'HAPPY BIRTHDAY MUM!' on it .

When Mum came downstairs, she sat down at the kitchen table and stared at it.

'Oh, George,' she said. 'Oh, George.' Then she started to cry.

Which almost made me wish I'd just given her a Mars bar, like last year.

'Prue and I have to go,' I said, hurriedly. It was true. I

needed Sir Crispin de-petrified before Miss Poker-Peagrim came home.

And I wanted to see what had come out of that egg.

CHAPTER SEVENTEEN

Big Nigel whickered when he saw Prudence, and came trotting up to the gate. He had company in his field today.

'It's the Vietnamese pot-bellied pig!' I said, as it oinked and grunted and butted the fence with a bristly snout. 'It's been de-petrified!'

It wasn't the only one.

The stable yard was full of life and noise – and animals. Dogs of all shapes and sizes were wagging their tails and barking their heads off. Cats of every colour were licking green slime out of their fur up in the branches of the tree, or on the stable roof, out of reach of the dogs. A family of guinea pigs was shrieking *wink-wink-wink* from inside a wooden crate, and an African Grey parrot had taken over one of Mrs Lind's hanging baskets, stamping his feet and squawking 'Give us a kiss! Give us a kiss!' over and over again.

Something small and fat with a curly tail came waddling

through the throng. It was Sir Crispin. He seemed pleased to see me, which was generous of him, considering it was sort of my fault that he had been turned into stone and used as a blunt instrument. I looked anxiously at his ear, but you could hardly tell where Mump's skull had chipped him.

Something else brushed against my leg. Next Door's Cat. He purred when I stroked him, before spitting at a yappy little Yorkshire terrier and leaping on to the roof of a familiar black van. Mump was sitting on the doorstep, eating a slice of cake.

'Nnngghh! Cake!' he said, waving at us.

'Hello!' said Mrs Lind, poking her head around a stable door. She was wearing an apron and had green smudges on her cheeks and on the tip of her nose. 'We're a bit overcrowded today. It seemed like a good idea to use the ointment before the smell got any worse. It's already put the ouroborus right off his porridge.'

'Where's Mortifer?' asked Prudence. We were wearing our sunglasses, just in case.

'In his stable,' said Mrs Lind. 'Sleeping off his adventures and rather a lot of curry. He was looking a bit thin, so Lo made a trip to the Star of India and ordered all his favourites. He's eaten a korma, a madras, a vindaloo, five helpings of peas pilau, sixteen onion bhajis and twenty-three poppadoms. The longer he stays asleep, the better. We can't let him out until we've got rid of this lot.' She waved a hand at the pack of animals. 'Some of the cats have already left. Cats always know where they're going. Lo will make sure the rest get home safely. It's best if he does it after dark. We don't want any awkward questions.'

I looked at the Jack Russell sniffing my trainers. It was Jamie May's Peanut. And there was Snuffy, the missing tabby cat I'd seen in the Sweet Shop window. 'You'd make a lot of money,' I said. 'if you claimed all the rewards people are offering to get their pets back.'

'What would I want a lot of money for?' said Mrs Lind. 'Money's like one of those annoying itches – the more you scratch, the itchier it gets. Once you start having a lot of it, you just want more. Stick to cake, is my advice, like Mr Mump over there. Mr Mump!' she called. 'Here's your cat – a little smelly, but good as new.'

Mump looked up from his slice of cake, his face splitting into a great big grin as Smelly Betty trotted towards him, her tail curled into a question mark.

'Nnnghh!' he said. 'Betty better!'

'That just leaves a couple of squirrels,' said Mrs Lind. 'And your friend.'

I'd forgotten about Crazy Daisy. Doom hadn't. The little dog was huddled against his mistress's stone feet, with his ears down flat and his tail between his legs.

'Oh, poor Doom!' said Prudence. 'Can we do Daisy next?'

'I'm afraid she may not be very pleased.' Mrs Lind looked anxious. 'I don't know what she's going to say …'

'I do,' I said. 'She'll say what she always says. The End of the World is upon us and we're all going to be eaten by the

Caterpillar.'

I was wrong. The first thing Daisy did, when Mrs Lind had towelled the ointment off her, was bend down rather stiffly and pat Doom. Then her eyes, as bright and beady as ever, fell on Mump, sitting on the doorstep with Smelly Betty on his lap and a plate of cake.

'Aha,' said Daisy. 'Cake. That's the ticket. Move up, big fellow.' And she sat down beside him.

Mump opened his mouth, then shut it again. 'Nnnghh,' he said, at last, and passed her the plate. 'Nnnghh *nnnghhh*!'

'Just what I was thinking,' agreed Daisy.

'Well, *that's* a relief,' said Mrs Lind. 'Whoops!' she added, as her foot caught the bucket of ointment, splashing one of the stone gryphons' tails. 'Mustn't waste it. Lo won't be pleased if he has to squeeze another weasel—'

She broke off, staring. We all stared. The gryphon's tail, smeared with green slime, had twitched. Without a word, Mrs Lind slopped on another dollop of ointment. The tail began to wave. Prudence and I both plunged our hands into the green gunge, not even caring about the smell as we plastered it over the two gryphons.

'Be careful,' warned Mrs Lind. 'Do the beaks last. They may be snappy.'

But the gryphons weren't interested in us. As we rubbed them down, they arched their backs, stretching like big cats, and preened each other's neck feathers. The bigger one cocked his leg on the stable door, while his mate scratched at a de-petrified flea. Then they began to play. Round and round the stable yard they went, in a mad game of Tag, scattering the other animals as they lolloped and leaped and spread their wings and soared. Daisy and Mump had frozen, mouthfuls of cake halfway to their lips.

'I wasn't expecting *that*!' admitted Mrs Lind. 'I wonder how long they've been trapped in stone. Centuries, probably.'

'They're certainly pleased to be free,' said Prudence, as we watched them skim the chimney pots.

At last the gryphons grew tired. The cats scattered, spitting with fright, as they flapped up into the tree, where they draped themselves gracefully over a branch and fell asleep. Once the show was over, Mump and Daisy blinked and went back to their cake.

'I wonder if those gryphons are a breeding pair?' mused Mrs Lind. 'It's a long time since we've had gryphon chicks at Wormestall. Speaking of chicks, I wonder if Dido and Lo are getting anywhere with that hatchling?'

What with Smelly Betty and Daisy and the gryphons, I'd forgotten about the hatchling.

'Where is it?' I asked. 'And *what* is it?'

Mrs Lind sighed. 'It's still in its egg. It's refusing to come out. Dido tried to help, but it just snapped at her. We've been trying to get it to eat, but it won't. Dido's brought it beetles and snails and worms from the garden. Lo's offered it mice and sausages and hot buttered toast. It's just not interested. Come and see.'

We followed her into the house, stepping over Daisy and

Mump, who seemed to be getting on very well. In the kitchen, Lo was on his knees, dangling a fish finger over the dog bed. Dido was beside him, cocking her head and clucking anxiously.

'Any luck?' asked Mrs Lind.

Lo shook his head.

I knelt down beside him. Dido gave me a half-hearted peck, but I ignored her.

'What's the matter with it?' I asked.

Lo hunched his shoulders. 'Don't ask me.'

I stared down at the egg. Zigzag cracks ran all over the marbled pink shell. The hole my shoe had made was bigger than yesterday – big enough for the little creature inside to push its snout out and flop, limply, over the edge. It was very pale, the colour of strawberry yogurt, and the ruby eye, which had fixed on mine so brightly, was gummy and dull. It wasn't making its *weep-weep* noise. It wasn't making any noise at all. I felt a knot tighten in my stomach. *This is your stupid fault,* I told myself. *Why did you have to go and put your big foot in it? You trod on it, and made it hatch too early, and now—*

'It's not going to *die*, is it?' Prudence was standing just behind me.

'No!' I said, desperately. 'No, it can't! It was fine yesterday! When I took it out of the bread bin, it looked right at me, cheeky as anything. And it was talking to me.'

'It's very weak,' said Mrs Lind, sadly. 'I'm afraid that it won't be long before— Wait a minute – *what* did you say,

George?'

There was nothing for it. I had to own up.

'It was when Diamond was here. Before she ... you know. Mingus exploded and everyone was barging about, trying to get out of the kitchen. I trod on the egg. I'm really, really sorry. It seemed to be all right, so I put it in the bread bin to keep it safe. I didn't want Diamond or Mintzer seeing it.'

'Let me get this straight,' said Mrs Lind. 'When the egg cracked, you were the only person in here? So you were the first living thing it saw?'

I nodded.

'That explains it, then,' said Mrs Lind. 'It's been pining.'

'Pining?' I frowned. 'What for?'

'You, George.' Lo was sitting back on his heels, grinning. 'It thinks you're its mother. Look, it's perking up already. Now that Mummy's back!'

It was true. There was a change. The creature stirred. The ruby eye blinked and rolled, seeking mine.

'What d'you mean?' I said.

'It's imprinted on you, George,' explained Mrs Lind, looking much more cheerful. 'A hatchling like this thinks the first living thing it sees must be its mother. The first person it saw was you, and now it's fixated. It expects you to feed it and look after it and teach it everything it needs to know. Nobody else will do. It's a big responsibility. You can accept it, or not. It's up to you. But if you don't, the hatchling will die.'

Weep-weep, peeped the hatchling, faintly.

'I accept.' I didn't even stop to think.

'Congratulations on your new baby, *Mummy*!' said Lo, and passed me the fish finger. 'You can try getting it to eat this, for starters.'

As soon as the baby saw me holding the fish finger, the *weep-weeps* grew louder and it tried to wriggle out of its shell, opening its jaws to show rows of tiny, pin-sharp teeth. A packet and a half of fish fingers later, it had crawled right out of its egg and was curled up in my lap. I stroked its scaly spine with one finger, wondering how I was going to smuggle it home and look after it without Mum realizing that there was an Unidentified Reptile in the house. And what was I going to feed it? Looking at those teeth, I guessed it didn't eat vegetables. Possibly it ate vegetarians.

'It's a pretty colour,' said Prudence. I could tell by her voice that she was a tiny bit jealous. 'Pink.'

I quoted Mum. 'Real men aren't afraid of pink,' I said, firmly.

'Hmm,' said Mrs Lind. 'I wonder. If that's what I think it is, then one day, when it grows up, Real Men are going to be very afraid of it indeed ...'

The very last of the De-petrifaction Ointment was used up on the two left-over squirrels.

'That's that,' said Mrs Lind, as the squirrels scampered away. 'I'll be glad to get rid of that smell!'

Lo raised his eyebrows at her. 'Aren't you forgetting something? Or ... somebody?'

For a moment, Mrs Lind looked puzzled, then she clapped her hand over her mouth.

'Numpty!' she exclaimed. 'How could I forget poor Numpty?' She peered into the empty bucket. 'There's not enough in there to de-petrify a mouse! What are we to do?'

'Nothing,' said Lo, yawning. 'Until I find another weasel. That could be ages.'

'I feel *very* guilty!' said Mrs Lind. 'Never mind. It can't be helped. I'll make more ointment – and a cake like he had on his birthday, with the fish-paste icing and the crystallized spiders on top.'

Everything went back to normal, but better.

Mrs Poker-Peagrim didn't notice the chip in Sir Crispin's ear. Neither she nor Frank ever guessed that he had spent the weekend turned to stone. Everyone at home was glad to see Next Door's Cat back in his place on the ironing board.

Mortifer showed no signs of wanting to run away again, and the gryphons settled in very quickly, although Mrs Lind complained that they took up the whole of the sofa and left feathers everywhere, as well as hairs.

Daisy and Doom didn't live in the park any more. The park people had been painting all the benches, and Daisy's had a sign on it that said 'Wet Paint – Do Not Touch', so she went to live with Mump and Prudence instead. Daisy didn't like the idea of walls and a roof – she said she was used to sleeping under the stars. Mump moved the sofa out into the garden for her, but she complained it was too soft and she couldn't get comfortable. Luckily, it turned out that while Daisy was petrified she had actually, finally, won the Lottery. She had enough money to buy a bench of her very own, and there was enough left over to buy a little tea shop too, where she and Mump were going to sell cake.

As for Mintzer, we dressed him in a flappy old raincoat and put him in the vegetable garden at the farm. He was supposed to scare the crows away, but he wasn't very good at it. Mostly they just perched on his head and pooed on him.

One morning, when Mrs Lind and I were doing the milking together, I tried asking her about Lo.

'It's true, isn't it, about him being a . . . you know what?'

Mrs Lind sat on the milking stool, her cheek resting against Mrs Wednesday's hairy flank as milk hissed into the bucket.

'Hmm?' was all she said.

I tried harder. 'The A word. It's true he's an A—' I hesitated, and lost my nerve. 'An Above-Average Flier?'

Mrs Lind smiled. 'He is, isn't he? Much too fast, of course – one of these days he's going to crash.'

'But what's he doing here? On earth? At Wormestall?'

Mrs Lind looked thoughtful. 'I suppose you could say he was on detention ...'

'Detention?' Mrs Tuesday's milk squirted all over my shoe. 'What for?'

'Speeding, mostly,' admitted Mrs Lind. 'Where he comes from, they're fussy about rules. You know Lo. He doesn't like being told what to do. There may have been more to it than that. He doesn't choose to talk about it, and it would be bad manners to press him.'

The hiss of milk stopped. Mrs Lind stood up, picking up her bucket and stool. I knew better than to ask any more questions.

I didn't have time to waste wondering about Lo. I was too busy looking after the hatchling. It's hard work, being something's mother, especially when you have to keep it a secret. I took it to school, zipped into my backpack, and never got to play football at Break any more because I had to lock us both in the toilet and stuff it full of food to keep it quiet until Lunch. Then I had to do the same thing at Lunch, to shut it up until Home Time. At home, it lived in the Emergency Bike Fund box under my bed. I had to stop Mum coming into my bedroom and poking about, which meant that I had to start making my bed and picking up my dirty socks and not leaving crumbs. I also had to set my alarm to go off every three hours at night, before the hatchling woke everybody up with its hungry *weep-weeping*. Most of my Wormestall wages went on fish fingers and meatballs. You have to make sacrifices when you're a parent.

It helped that Mum was in a good mood. She had a new mermaid to replace the one Doom chewed up. Mump made it. He shut himself up in the Stuffing Room and wouldn't come out, even for cake. Then he turned up at The Mermaid's Cave one day and put it in the window. It had a proper silvery fish's tail (I recognized half the Piano Tuna), long, slippery green hair, and a surprised expression on its face. It was really rather pretty.

In an evil-step-mermaid sort of way.

Mum was thrilled.

'*So* much better than that sad old thing I had before!' she said, happily. 'It's so lifelike!'

'*Too* lifelike,' said Prudence, with a shiver. 'It gives me the creeps.'

She had locked the doors to the Trophy Room, and hidden the keys somewhere only she knew. The 'dragon' in the Stuffing Room had had a proper burial in the orchard at Wormestall and we'd planted flowers on its grave. As for St George, he turned out to be a stuffed baboon.

'Nobody hurt it. Its name was Biff and it died peacefully of old age in the zoo,' Daisy assured us. 'Mump said so.'

We were all around Mrs Lind's kitchen table, having tea. Everyone looked at Daisy in surprise.

'Did Mump really say all that?' asked Prudence, impressed. 'And you understood him?'

'Of course,' said Daisy. 'I understand everything he says. The rest of you just don't listen properly.'

Dido was on her eggs. Tail-biter was sucking his tail on the rocking chair. Prudence was feeding the Ping Feng piglet which was growing fast. (Lo had been heard muttering about sausages and bacon. Mrs Lind promised us he was only joking, but I wasn't so sure.) The hatchling was on my lap, working its way through a plate of ham and cheese sandwiches. I hoped the Ping Feng hadn't noticed the ham. Mump had popped upstairs to visit the kraken. (He had the hang of it now, and kept fish fingers in his pocket like the rest of us.)

'Daisy?' I had to ask. 'Is the End of the World still coming?'

'I expect so,' she said, cutting another slice of cake. 'But it doesn't matter much. I'll tell you a secret, George. There's no point in worrying about the End because, really, there's no such thing. The end of one thing, you'll find, is always the beginning of another ...'

THE END

THE ANIMALS OF WORMESTALL FARM

THE EXTINCT ONES
(Lingerlings)

ARCHAEOPTERYX (ar-kee-op-ter-ix – 'ancient wing')
Extinct 150 million years. Looks like a bird, but with claws on the end of its wings, and a beak full of teeth. Not very good at flying, especially taking off and landing.

AUROCHS (or-ox – Mrs Tuesday and Mrs Wednesday)
Extinct since 1627. Long before that, found their way into prehistoric cave paintings. Enormous wild cows, with ferocious horns. Not keen on being milked. Hunted to extinction by humans.

BULLOCKORNIS
(bull-ock-orn-iss – 'ox bird' – Donald and Jemima)
Extinct 15 million years. Nicknamed 'Demon Ducks of Doom'. Taller than a man (2.5 metres), they can't fly but run fast, and enjoy ripping up meat with their heavy, curved beaks. Any meat will do. They're not fussy, but they don't like bread. They prefer boy.

DODO (Didus Ineptus – 'stupid dodo' – Dido)
Extinct since 1681. Fat, flightless birds, with tails like feather dusters. Dodos were perfectly happy minding their own business on the island of Mauritius until humans arrived in 1598 and spoiled it all. Dido guards her egg collection fiercely – even though they weren't laid by her.

EARLY MAMMAL (Mingus)
Not properly extinct. First appeared about 210 million years ago and has been evolving ever since into the mammals around today. Small hairy things, like sabre-tooth squirrels, they scurried about between the dinosaurs' feet. Those that didn't get trodden on, or eaten, survived when the dinosaurs died out – which proves that Bigger is not always Better.

EOHIPPUS
(ee-oh-hipp-us – 'dawn horse')
Extinct 50 million years. Pygmy pony, about the size of a spaniel, with toes.

ICHTHYOSAUR
(ick-thee-oh-sor – 'fish lizard')
Extinct 90 million years. Looks like a dolphin, but with a long jaw full of very sharp teeth.

THE OTHER ONES
(Cryptids)
Serious, sensible people say these animals do not exist. Serious, sensible people are very often right. But not always.

BASILISK (Mortifer)
A giant serpent with a mane of feathers and a beaked nose. His breath is so bad it shrivels vegetables, and any creature that meets his eyes is instantly petrified (turned into stone). It's not his fault. He can't help it.

DRACUNCULUS DENTATUS
(small toothed dragon)
Mrs Lind's Great Aunt Hepzibah met one of these in the shrubbery, after which she needed the Emergency Wooden Leg. It was the dragon that was small, not the teeth.

GRYPHON
Front end of an eagle, rear end of a lion. When not chasing pigeons (or wildebeest, if available), they like to lie around in trees. This can end badly for unsuspecting passers-by. (Note: always check for gryphons before walking under a tree.)

DRAGON (Grissel)
Many different varieties, including Grissel's draco britannicus. Some are more dangerous than others. All are best treated with respect. Once upon a time, Grissel met St George. She didn't like him.

KRAKEN
Like an octopus, or squid, the kraken is a cephalopod (which means 'head-foot'). One day, Mrs Lind's kraken will be the size of a small island, big enough to sink a cruise-ship with one tentacle. For now, it mostly lives in the toilet. Partial to fish fingers.

OUROBOROS (Tail-biter)
A dragon-like creature that spends all eternity sucking its own tail. It's a boring job, but somebody has to do it, or Time will stop. Inclined to gloom, it likes rocking chairs, but not being sat-upon.

PING FENG
(Crackling Rose and piglets)
Black pig, with a head at both ends. This can lead to difficulties if the heads want to go in opposite directions.

UNICORN (Big Nigel)
NOT the airy-fairy, shimmery-shiny, pearly-horned sort that farts rainbows. Nigel is the Heavy Horse of the unicorn world, and gets very grumpy about having his tail combed or his horn grated (for alicorn – a miracle medicine that cures almost anything).